The 200th Messiah

by

Chayym Zeldis

iUniverse, Inc.
New York Bloomington

The 200th Messiah

iUniverse books may be ordered through booksellers or by contacting:

iUniverse
1663 Liberty Drive
Bloomington, IN 47403
www.iuniverse.com
1-800-Authors (1-800-288-4677)

ISBN: 978-0-595-48601-4 (pbk)
ISBN: 978-0-595-49529-0 (cloth)
ISBN: 978-0-595-60694-8 (ebk)

Printed in the United States of America

For my wife, Nina, in love and gratitude …

And in loving memory of Jerzy Kosinski,
comrade-in-arms

He who is kind to the cruel ends by being cruel to the kind.

—Midrash

Afterward, after it had happened, Tate tried to remember exactly how it was. More accurately, he wanted to know whether in that fateful split second he had seen it coming, or somehow perceived or sensed it, or whether he had actually caught sight of it on its way—or whether he'd had no knowledge or inkling of it, and it had come like a bolt out of the blue. It seemed important for Tate to know, because for a time he kept blaming himself, kept telling himself there was something he could have done to prevent it, to change things. Some action he could have taken. Could at the very least have warned her; could have shoved her aside; could even have interposed himself, his body and skull, between her and it. Blaming himself altered nothing. Guilt made no difference. Reconstructing it in any way other than the way in which it had occurred was sheer fantasy. Useless, profitless, painful, baiting fantasy. It had happened as it had happened. *Period.*

Alan and Margie Tate had turned. To edge their way through the Arab crowd and cross Salah-ed-Din Street and go through the Jaffa Gate and back to the Tower of David Museum. And the stone came streaking down. Who had thrown it? Man, woman—child? What difference. A human hand unleashed it. Tate heard before he saw. Heard it strike. The sound. That sickening sound of rock against skull. Of splintering bone. He heard and would never forget. Would never erase. Then his head flicked and he saw—

The stone was finished. Had done its work. Was dropping. Margie was dropping. Her head was twisted aside; her knees had buckled. *And the blood!* The blood was everywhere, everywhere he looked. But where in God's name was it from? Blood on the front of her dress. On the collar. Splashed over the purse that was slipping from her crooked shoulder. Even her shoes, her pale blue walking shoes, the ones she'd bought especially for the trip, were spattered with it. *So much blood!* And so red, so incredibly red—a red it seemed he'd never seen before, a red that did not, that could not exist in nature! Yet there it was. The red of her blood. *Margie's.* Everywhere he looked and did not want to see. Did not believe. Where was it from? Why couldn't someone tell him where it was from?

Then Tate saw. Saw as she slipped downward, a lost, limp store dummy painted with blood; saw as he reached for her, lunged for what was left of her. Her head. Her temple. Her right temple. Or where her right temple had caved in. The blood was welling, surging from the staved-in skull, the shattered bone, the cavity. *A giant, oozing carnation that did not stop blossoming.*

Then Tate had her in his arms. Her weight. Her body. Her oozing life. He gagged. Her body swayed with his. The two of them were a pendulum, swaying in the street. He could not hold her, yet he had to hold her. She was his. He wanted her. He would never give her up. "Oh, God," he cried out: "Somebody help! Somebody help us!" But nobody came near. In fact, everyone was running away, in the opposite direction. *Kaffias* and robes and *yashmaks*—all running, all fleeing. "Oh, God," he screamed. *"See what they've done! Just see what they've done!"*

Everything whirled. Spun around. The vacant, dirt-smudged sidewalk that had emptied of Arabs. The Old City walls across the street. The shops and stalls on this side. Everything raced, spun, dipped. He felt the nausea. Saw the black spots. Before his eyes the spots that were as black as the blood was red. He would not last. He was going down with her. There was nobody to lift them, to save them. They were lost. Lost to darkness. The sky was only a flash, and then it shut out. *He shut out.*

* * *

When he opened his eyes, Tate saw the metal brightness of the sky. He thought it was a mirror and could not understand why he didn't see his own reflection. And then he realized he was lying on the sidewalk, looking up. All around him, there was a tremendous hubbub: wailing sirens, people shouting at each other in a language he couldn't understand, somebody—a child—crying. Three people bent over him: two men and a woman, all in uniforms. He had no idea who they were or why he was on the sidewalk. Had he been injured? Was he ill? Was he alive, even? Or was he dead and in some crazy, afterlife place? One of the men and then the woman spoke to him. "I don't … understand," he muttered.

"English?"

"What?"

"English," said the woman. "Do you speak English, sir?"

"Yes, English, please." Tate said. And then, struck with sudden horror, he said, "Where's Sarah? Has something … happened to her?"

"Are you hurt, sir?" the woman asked.

"Sarah," Tate persisted. "What happened to her? Where is she?"

One of the men—he had a thick, black mustache and wore sergeant's stripes on his sleeve—grasped Tate's shoulder. "Sarah is the lady who was hit by the rock?"

And then Tate knew. It was not his daughter, Sarah, who had been killed years ago in a car accident. It was not Sarah who had been hit by the rock now. *It was his wife.* "Oh, my God!" he cried out. "Margie—it's *Margie*!" He struggled to get up. The sergeant and the other policeman helped him. "Where is she?" Tate asked hoarsely.

He got to his feet and leaned unsteadily on the sergeant. Three mounted policemen and perhaps a dozen on foot kept the crowd back. Green-bereted border policemen and soldiers with leveled weapons fanned out over the sidewalks. Traffic was completely halted, and there were several jeeps and command cars in the cleared area. The sergeant escorted Tate slowly forward.

The ambulance doors were wide open; two attendants in white were just sliding the stretcher in. Margie was covered with a blanket—someone had covered her, just as he'd covered her the night before in their room. Her head was swathed in white bandage through which the blood had stubbornly begun to seep; her face was a clay mask. Tate scarcely recognized her. "I—I'm her husband," he said.

"Please get in," said one of the attendants.

Jerusalem, December 24, 1992
Mt. Zion Hospital
1:33 pm

While Margie was in the emergency room, Tate was interrogated by the police out in the corridor. "Did you see who threw the rock?" the officer asked.

"No."

"Are you certain?"

Tate nodded. "But—it seemed to fall."

"To fall?" The officer raised a hand above his head and made a downward motion.

"Yes."

"It was probably from a rooftop. The Arabs throw rocks down at the Jews. There have been several incidents in the last few days." The policeman cleared his throat. "But someone who saw the Arab throw the stone has already come forward; we have a description, and we'll be looking—"

Tate said nothing.

"I'm sorry," said the officer. "I'm very sorry this happened. I wish your wife a speedy and full recovery."

"Thanks," said Tate.

Margie had been brought to the emergency room around one; about an hour after that, she went up to the operating room. Tate waited down in the lobby. He paced the marble floor interminably. He watched other people pace and smoke and squirm in their seats and gape like fish out of water when they dropped off into unexpected sleep. After a couple of hours, he bought a cheese sandwich and coffee from dispensing machines. He took two or three bites of the sandwich and threw the rest away in disgust but drank the coffee. He spoke to no one, except now and then to a hospital information person for news of the operation's progress, when there was any. He waited. The old, isolated, straightjacket-self-Tate waited. He did not speculate or hope or plan; he did not even think. He kept control of himself. *He kept control of control.*

* * *

Margie had been taken to the operating room at about two. She came out at a quarter to five in the afternoon, and went into the recovery room. Tate got permission to go in and see her for a short while. He stood stiffly by the bed and murmured a few words of love. And he prayed briefly, asking that she live and return to him. Then he went out and sat on a bench in the corridor in silence. Cold, stony, regulated silence. A file of nurses and interns in white, looking like ghosts, passed continually before him. One young nurse stopped several times to ask if she could bring him anything or help him in any way. He shook his head. He kept his vigil. And his silence.

When next he looked at his watch, it was ten past six. He thought that he ought to sleep. He needed the rest, had to have it if he were to function. And it was imperative for him to function. Margie needed him; he needed to be there for her. He would make himself a machine: a function machine. He closed his eyes. He opened them again when someone spoke to him. "Eh?" he muttered, waking from a dream too terrible to remember .

"Mr. Tate?"

"Yes. What time is it?"

The man in the white jacket standing in front of him smiled. "It's five to eight," he said: "I'm Dr. Elfenbaum. Can we speak?"

Tate nodded. He followed the doctor down the corridor to a small conference room. Elfenbaum opened the door. "Please," he said. "Go right in and have a seat."

"You speak English so well," said Tate: "You're from England?"

"South Africa," said Elfenbaum.

He was a man of about Tate's height, but of a heavier build. Although he looked no more than fifty, his thick shock of hair had gone altogether white. Folding his long-fingered hands on his lap, he said, "As I told you, Mr. Tate, my name is Elfenbaum. Moshe Elfenbaum. I'm the neurosurgeon in charge of your wife's case. I'm the one who operated on your wife this afternoon."

"How how is she?"

"Her condition is very serious. I'm certain you realize that." Elfenbaum unclasped his hands and laid them limply on the table. "The rock that struck your wife was thrown from a considerable height. It fractured her skull. There has been a bleed in, and damage to, both the occipital and parietal lobes."

"What does that mean?"

"It means, I'm afraid, that your wife has sustained injury to her vision and her speech. We don't as yet know the full extent of the damage. But if she survives—"

"If?"

Elfenbaum touched the tips of his fingers together. "Right at this moment, the brain continues to fill with fluid; we evacuate it. She may require further surgery—we'll have to wait and see." He cleared his throat. "If your wife survives, Mr. Tate, she may very well be blind or speech-impaired."

"I understand."

"On the positive side, we've stabilized her vital signs. We'll be able to move her to the ICU ward in a bit. She's in a coma. But patients do come out of comas—and there's a chance your wife may. She needs stimulation. All the stimulation she can get. The radio. And personal contact—that's even more important. Read to her. Talk to her. Try to reach her, to bring her back. Don't let up. It may succeed. Who can say?"

"I understand."

"I'm relying on you."

Tate nodded.

Elfenbaum was silent for a moment. Then he said, "I—well, I just want to say that I'm very sorry this happened, Mr. Tate."

"I'm sure you are."

"We'll do our very best—I promise you that. And if there's anything you wish to know, anything I can explain or clear up for you, please feel free to consult me."

"I will. Thank you."

Both men rose. With Elfenbaum leading, they left the conference room. In the corridor, Elfenbaum extended a hand, and Tate took it. *It was a hand steered by God, he thought.*

Jerusalem, December 25
Mt. Zion Hospital
2:25 pm

Early in the afternoon, they moved Margie to the ICU ward. The large room, sectioned off by curtains to make private cubicles, was flooded with the sunshine of another bright December day. On the radio, whose volume had been turned up, a woman with a throaty voice was singing a popular tune. Tate turned to the nurse. "She—my wife—likes classical music." he said. "Would you please?"

"Of course," said the nurse: "I'll change the station. Imm—imm—" She looked over at Tate for help.

"Immediately."

"Immed-iately. Yes. Thank you." As she twisted the radio's dial, the nurse smiled. "I will speak to your wife in English. I wish to improve my English."

Tate parted the curtains of Margie's cubicle. He closed them and went over to the bed. "Hello, darling," he said slowly, earnestly, marshalling his will. "Do you hear? Do you hear the music? It's Sibelius. The Third. For you—" He stared down at the expressionless face and the tubes. "Margie," he said. "I'll bring lots of tapes. Everything you love. We'll listen to it together, the two of us." He reached down and lightly ran his fingers over the grayish skin of her frail forearm. "I want you back, Margie, and I know that you want to come back. We'll work it out; we'll make it happen. When the two of us work together, we're an unbeatable combination—you know that!" *An unbeatable combination.* It was a little private saying they'd used at times of crisis since the earliest days of their marriage.

Outside the cubicle, he called to the nurse. "Miss!"

"My name is Tova."

"Miss—Tova, I—I'm going to leave now. I need to take care of some matters. I'll come back just as soon as I can. In the meantime—"

The nurse, raven-haired and overweight, nodded. "Don't worry, Mr. Tate, your wife is … in good hands—is that the expression?"

"Yes."

"We'll take the very best care of her."

He didn't like leaving Margie, even "in good hands." But it was necessary, and he'd do whatever was necessary. He'd made up his mind, set his will. He was the function machine.

Back in the hotel room, he undressed and shaved and took a shower. He put on fresh underwear and fresh clothing—the shirt and pants he'd worn had spots of Margie's blood on them. Leaning in toward the mirror above the dresser, he saw the scrubbed, clean-shaven face of the function machine. He ran a comb through his hair several times and peered at the reflection again. The mouth was pinched and the eyes were dead. But it was fine; the face would pass muster.

Down in the lobby, he thought, *Eat. Better eat. The function machine needs fuel. Every machine does.* He went directly to the coffee shop and seated himself in a secluded corner and ordered supper. A hamburger steak and French fries and salad, seeded rolls and coffee. He meant well but ran into trouble. Repeatedly, the food rose on him and he had to force it back down.

"Some more coffee, sir?" asked the waiter.

He shook his head. "No. Please bring the check. I'm in a hurry."

The doorman got him a taxi, which left him off in the center of the city. He went into an electronics store for a tape recorder and into an adjacent record store for tapes. Halfway down the block was a large bookstore. He entered, passed quickly along the shelves and brought a dozen books to the counter. "Are they a gift?" asked the clerk. "Shall I wrap them?"

"They're a gift," said Tate. "But you needn't wrap them."

*   *   *

He snapped the lid of the cassette chamber shut and pressed the play button. As the music spilled out, he watched her face for some evidence that she recognized it.

Nothing.

"Margie," he said to her, "it's Beethoven's Ninth. You know it. You love it. We used to listen to it all the time. Listen to it now, Margie. Show me that you hear it."

Nothing.

If she heard it, she gave no sign. If she knew he was there—if she knew at all—she made no response. If she wasn't there, he wondered, then where was she? In another world? Or in some limbo between this one and that? He leaned over her. "Margie," he whispered, "where are you?" He bent over still closer, so that his lips all but touched her ear. "It really doesn't matter where you are, darling. Just come back to me."

Nothing.

He stood by her. She was plaster face mask and tubes and support-system monitors and white sheets and whiter nurses circling like moths. She was a shell left empty by its tenant on the sand; she was an abandoned shipwreck. She was his. She was his, and he stood by her, and the music played. She remained silent, and he remained silent, and Beethoven spoke. When it came time for the "Ode to Joy," he trembled. "Margie," he told her, "Beethoven was beating against brick with bare hands. The bricks have fallen. He's beginning to soar. Do you hear?"

Nothing.

"The 'Ode to Joy,'" he said. "We used to listen together. We used to sing. Remember how we used to sing?" As if the music were lifting him, he straightened up. "Want to sing now, Margie? Come on, Margie, sing with me."

He had trembled. Now, the dam burst. He spread his arms and let the flood rip out. That was it. Beethoven and he had soared above the debris, the refuse, the offal of the world. The next thing he knew, the curtain around the cubicle was parted. Two nurses were at his sides. They seemed disturbed. And there was an intern as well—a tall, gangling, pale-skinned fellow who looked like a fugitive from *Ichabod Crane. Praise God Bearbones*, thought Tate, who was almost amused. The intern was talking, talking, talking, but what the devil did he want? One of the nurses shook Tate by the shoulder and that did the trick; he heard her.

"Mr. Tate, Mr. Tate!"

"Huh?"

"Mr. Tate, please!"

"What … is it? What's wrong?"

"It's after eleven. You're singing at the top of your lungs. The other patients—"

Tate shivered.

"This is a hospital, Mr. Tate. We have rules."

"Of course."

The mingled disbelief and annoyance left the nurse's light-brown eyes. "You look exhausted, Mr. Tate. Why don't you go home and get a good night's sleep and come back in the morning? What do you say, Mr. Tate?"

"Of course."

* * *

He decided that he would walk back to the hotel. The streets were all but deserted, and it seemed as if he had Jerusalem all to himself. It was much colder than it had been on previous nights and he was wearing only a light jacket, but he didn't mind. The chill, the bluish light of the street lamps, and the stone buildings seemed to numb the edge of his weariness. At the entrance to the hotel, he stood for a time with his hands in his pockets, staring up at the host of stars chiseled into the black sky. They told him nothing—not that he had bothered himself to ask. He remained there, his teeth beginning to chatter, until a man in a button-down sweater and peaked cap came up to him. "Want a taxi, sir?" Tate shook his head and went into the lobby.

As he passed the reception desk, the clerk—a skinny, young fellow from Paris with whom he and Margie had chatted amiably several times—called out, "Mr. Tate … Mr. Tate!"

Tate halted. "Did you want me?"

"Yes, yes, Mr. Tate. I have something here for you." He turned to the rows of cubby holes behind him. "Here," he said, turning back to Tate who had come over to the counter. "This came for you about an hour ago. I tried your room, but no one was in."

Tate took the envelope with the telegram inside. "Thanks," he murmured.

"You're welcome."

Tate did not open the envelope. Inside the room, he laid it on the dresser. He hung his jacket in the closet—out of deference to Margie's penchant for neatness—and then went into the bathroom, where he washed up. The curtains were pulled back, and when he came out, he stared over the terrace at the sky and wondered if God ever counted the stars? Then he sat down and called room service. He ordered a tuna salad sandwich and juice; an older man, wearing a toupee, brought the food. Tate managed to eat the entire sandwich, and he drank half the pitcher of orange juice.

Suddenly, Dr. Hadashi's face came to him. He was the psychiatrist whom Margie and Tate had met in the Israel Museum several days after they'd arrived. A kindly, soft-spoken, charming man with penetrating electric-blue eyes who had helped them look for Margie's lost contact lens and then conversed with them over coffee in the museum cafeteria for some hours. Tate remembered how the psychiatrist had described visiting friends in a kibbutz called Nof Ginossar, on the shore of the Sea of Galilee, which was the *Yam Kinneret* in Hebrew, its name deriving from the word *kinor*, or violin, because it was shaped like one. "Jesus's territory," Tate had thought at the time. And Tate recalled Dr. Hadashi's warm and promising handshake when they parted. At that moment, Tate had sensed the possibility of a deep relationship between them. Perhaps the doctor could be of help now? So Tate pulled the phone over and extended a finger to dial, but found he'd forgotten the number, though he had promised himself to remember it in the cafeteria. He fished Hadashi's calling card from his wallet and dialed. No answer. Maybe he'd dialed wrong? He tried again and let the phone ring perhaps twenty times. Still no answer. He hung up and pushed the food trolley back. Then he rose, went over to the dresser, and picked up the envelope. He opened it, unfolded the telegram, and, standing where he was, read:

> *SINCE HE WAS UNABLE TO LOCATE YOU YOUR BROTHER-IN-LAW REACHED ME THROUGH THE CHURCH GROUP AND REQUESTED I CONTACT YOU. REGRET TO INFORM YOU YOUR SISTER JENNIFER PASSED AWAY YESTERDAY AT 4 P.M. MY DEEPEST CONDOLENCES. MAY THE LORD HAVE MERCY ON HER SOUL.*
> *REVEREND ANDREW SPERRIS*

Tate remained for a time with the telegram in his hand and then put it back on the dresser. He sat on the bed. His sister was gone. No knot of pain tied up his heart. He had never loved her; he could not mourn her. Long ago, in earliest childhood, she had signed herself over to their father. They had always been a pair. Two scorpions. God took one; now, He'd taken the other. Tate was struck by a thought. His fingers dug into the bedspread. That was it! God's arithmetic. The way it worked. He had claimed Jennifer; surely, He was going to spare Margie! It couldn't be clearer, more logical: *God had canceled Alan Tate's sister and would restore his wife to perfect health.*

Tate lay back on the bed. He intended to remain calm, not to give expression to his elation. He would make his mind a refrigerator, his heart a freezer. Just stay calm and collected. Let God do His work in peace. That was the way. Keep what he knew a secret between him and God. Not tell anybody. Not even drop a hint. Just carry on. Do what the doctor had told him. Keep the function machine chugging. Put on a face. Keep up the act. Let the world think what it wanted. While he, Tate, really knew the outcome.

He closed his eyes. But sleep wouldn't come. He was bone-weary, wiped out, but he couldn't sleep. It was unbearable, unfair. He could no longer stand being awake. He wanted to, had to shut everything out. Had to turn out the light in his mind. Gritting his teeth, he roused himself and got up. He went to the little cabinet next to the closet and broke the seal and took out four minibottles of scotch. He turned over a clean tumbler and poured the scotches one after the other into it; he got the pitcher from the trolley and filled the glass to its brim with orange juice. Then he tilted his head back and drank it off.

The last thing he remembered was flopping onto the bed. "Thank you, Jennifer," he mumbled, "for finally doing something decent—" And then the liquor hit him.

Jerusalem, December 26, 1992
Hilton Hotel
6:10 am

Tate opened his eyes. The daylight that streamed in through the parted curtains was battleship-gray. Blinking, he sat up on the bed. His head seemed to be filled with cobweb, his mouth was dry, and his tongue felt like a wad of cotton. Slowly, he got to his feet. He started for the bathroom, but his reflection in the mirror stopped him. His hair was disheveled, his face was unshaven, his clothing was rumpled. He looked—he thought groggily—as if he'd spent a night "on Bald Mountain." He glanced to the left and caught sight of the telegram. His heart filled with elation and certainty: Jennifer condemned, Margie reprieved. *An equation from on high.*

He took a cold shower and then a hot one. He put on clean clothes— gray pants, a navy-blue turtleneck, and a gray-tweed sports jacket, all of which Margie'd picked out for him and were her favorites. In the coffee shop, he had a mushroom omelet, a mountainous Middle East salad, and two rolls. He washed it all down with three cups of steaming coffee. He had really stoked the function machine's furnace and was duly satisfied. Today, there would be a turn for the better. He sensed it. He smelled victory in the air, and he could not be mistaken.

He arrived at the hospital at eight fifteen. One of the elevators was out of service, and it took him nearly ten minutes to get upstairs. He could not wait to get to the ICU ward; he was convinced that good news awaited him. But the nurse on duty—he thought her name was Shira, something like that—was matter-of-fact. "No change," she told him curtly.

"Are you certain?"

The nurse bristled. "Of course I'm certain."

He didn't argue, but he didn't believe her, didn't give a damn what she said. There had to be some improvement. She just hadn't paid sufficient attention, hadn't noticed it—that was all. He hurried directly over to Margie's bed and peered down. Wasn't there a break in the gray pallor? A hint of color in her cheeks? In her lips? He examined her more closely. Of course, there was improvement, however minute. No one, he decided, except he, had observed it. He grimaced. It wasn't his fault if they didn't pay proper attention!

He pulled over a chair and sat by the bed. "Margie," he said in a low voice, so that he would not be overheard. "None of them here knows it yet, but you're on your way back; you're going to recover." He lowered his voice still more. "Margie, God has given me a sign. I know you don't believe in such things, but it's really happened. Trust me. I can't tell you what the sign is now; that's confidential, strictly between me and God. But you're coming out of this. I know for a fact."

He reached through the rails and picked up her hand. Tiny. Birdlike. The skin almost translucent. Lifeless. That was all right. It didn't shock him, didn't agitate him, didn't worry him. Things would be different. "Now, listen," he told her. "On the way over to the hospital this morning, I decided that I'd tell you the story of my life. Isn't that a good idea? Well, I thought you'd like it. I'm going to start with my earliest memories, the very first things I recall, and continue on up to the present. I'll describe everything exactly as I remember having lived it, as 'objectively' as I can. *The Complete, Unabridged, Unexpurgated Story of Alan Tate, Your Loving Husband.* And—and when I get to the point where we are now, you—you'll wake up, you'll come back." He wet his lips. "OK? Agreed? Ready? Here I go!"

* * *

And so he began. From the beginning. He tried to omit nothing and—harder still—to distort nothing. He spoke in his usual voice, but it sounded to his ears somehow altered. He realized that what he heard was the tone of anticipated triumph. God had formulated the deal, and would now work His wonders. Tate fully expected the resurrection of his wife from her deathbed. He could even be calm about it. His job was to talk; Margie's job was to listen; God's part was to bring her back …

Tate had been talking for a little more than an hour when it happened. The fingers he held in his came alive. He felt them move; *he actually felt them move!* For a moment, he stopped breathing. Was it true? Had he imagined it? Dreamed it? Wished it into actuality? No, there it was again. The movement. Her fingers really moved! *And this time, they exerted pressure; they squeezed his own!* His heart raced, pounded at his ribs. He hadn't even gotten up to the present in his story; God had jumped the gun! Tears came to his eyes. "Margie," he whispered: "Darling … oh, my darling!"

Wait until the doctor heard!

* * *

At the very end of the corridor was a small alcove with a window that looked east to the mountains, along with several rattan chairs upholstered in a floral pattern. Dr. Elfenbaum gestured. "Please have a seat—"

Tate shook his head.

The doctor folded his arms across his white jacket. "Now, describe to me once again just what happened."

Tate did, precisely and in detail. When he finished, he said: "She's coming out of the coma, isn't she? I'm right, am I not, doctor?"

Elfenbaum let his arms drop; he tucked one hand into a pocket. He was silent for a moment. Then, in a quiet voice, he said, "It's hard to say. I understand your elation—I can relate to it very well—but I'm afraid I can't give you the news you want, the news we're all looking for."

"What do you mean? She squeezed my hand! I told you—"

Elfenbaum took Tate's arm. "Listen," he said. "The pressure you felt from her hand may very well be a positive sign, the heralding of recovery—or it may simply be an automatic reflex. At this point, we don't know which."

"But she must be getting well, doctor," Tate protested, conscious of the alarm and ire in his voice. "She *must*. You see, God is bending the bar of fate."

"What's that?"

"Nothing," said Tate, "nothing ..."

Elfenbaum released his hold on Tate's arm. "Look," he said, with obvious intent to reassure, "your wife's vital signs are stable—and that's what to be grateful for. As for recovery, well ... only time will tell the story."

Tate said nothing. There was an awkward silence, but Tate let the physician go without a word and without shaking his hand. Elfenbaum walked swiftly down the corridor and disappeared around a corner. Tate turned to the window. The day was heavily overcast, with massive clouds hanging over the mountains. He stood there, his jaw set, staring out. What did Elfenbaum know? What did any of them know? He thought of Margie's hand squeezing his. He remembered exactly how her fingers felt. He smiled. Beyond the cloud formations was God. Like a circus strongman, *He was bending the iron bar of fate!*

* * *

Tate spent the entire day telling Margie the story of his life. He sat by the bed and talked. When he tired, he played music on the tape recorder, sometimes humming along with the passages his wife loved best. He kept her hand in his, but what he waited for and fully expected did not come. He got nothing in return for what he gave. Not the twitch of a finger, not the flicker of an eyelid—nothing at all. With an eerie suddenness, daylight faded from the room. He glanced at his watch. Twenty past five. His voice was giving out, and he had a blinding headache. He put her hand down gently on the sheet and rose. "I'll be back," he said to the nurse.

"Are you leaving the building?"

"No. Why do you ask?"

The nurse shrugged. "It's a habit of mine ..."

"I'll be in the cafeteria," said Tate.

The cafeteria, usually crowded and smoke-filled, was almost deserted. An old woman with a kerchief on her head ate soup, bending her face to the plate; two young men in soiled jackets picked French fries from a cardboard container; a busboy was absently removing litter and leftovers from the tables. Tate selected the most remote place he could find and put his tray down. Mechanically, he chewed the egg salad sandwich, grinding his teeth into the crisp roll. "God will do it," he thought: "I know God will do it." He lifted the paper cup and sipped the coffee. "That's the bargain ..."

He was just draining his cup when the announcement came over the public address system.

"Mr. Alan Tate. Mr. Alan Tate!"

He was so busy plotting with God that he did not hear it the first time. It came again.

"Mr. Alan Tate. Please come to the ICU ward at once. Mr. Alan Tate!"

He caught the tail end of it—his name—and then the entire announcement when it was repeated for the third time. He set his cup on the tray and rose. "Calm," he thought. "Calm. That's the formula." The booming PA voice followed him to the door. "Easy does it," he thought, heading toward the elevators, "*Nice and easy. God is at the helm.*" He waited patiently. He let everyone else into the elevator ahead of him. As they went up, he whistled a bit of a Mozart piano sonata, the last thing he'd played for Margie before he went to supper.

Dr. Elfenbaum was waiting at the nurses' station. "Tate," he called out warmly, "we've been looking for you—"

"Here I am."

The doctor's rugged features looked relaxed. He smiled. "We have some good news for you, Tate."

"What ... news?"

"Mrs. Tate—your wife—has regained consciousness."

Tate wet his dry lips. "Margie's out of the coma? She's awake?"

Elfenbaum nodded. "She is! Definitely! I spoke to her not more than ten minutes ago."

Tate turned toward the door to the ward. "I must see her—"

But Elfenbaum caught his arm as he stepped forward. "One moment," he said firmly. "This development has been nothing short of, well, miraculous. However, I must caution you. We're not out of the woods yet. Remember that."

Tate scarcely heard him. He shook off the restraining grip and rushed through the door and into the ward. There were several nurses and interns at Margie's bedside. They moved away as Tate approached. He grasped the cold metal railing of the bed and looked down. Margie looked back up at him. He reached down and took her responsive hand. Then he bowed his head.

When he finished his prayer, he looked at his wife again. Her skin had lost some of its ashen pallor; he thought he could even discern a trace of color in her cheeks and in her parted lips. But the main thing, the glorious thing, was her eyes. They were wide open, blue as a seascape, and infinitely alive. He seemed to fall into them—to find in them all that he had lost, all that he had despaired of recovering. "Margie," he murmured, "my own …" Tenderly, he squeezed her hand, and she returned the pressure. "Margie, darling, it's so good … so good …"

"Alan—"

Her voice made him shiver. "You're back, Margie—you're really back! I—I've missed you terribly."

"Dearest Alan … I'm very glad … to see … you …" She spoke with difficulty, and her words were somewhat slurred, but he understood everything she said. "Even though," she continued, "you—you're a bit fuzzy."

He shook his head. "Don't worry about that, Margie," he told her. "Don't give it another thought. The doctor said it might be that way at first. But it'll pass. This—is only the beginning, the blessed beginning. You'll keep improving; you'll be completely well. We'll be together again."

"Alan—" But her voice trailed off into indistinguishable sounds. She could not finish.

Elfenbaum was at the bedside now. "She's tired out, Tate. She needs to rest."

"Yes, of course. To rest …"

"You can come back in the morning, first thing."

"Yes, yes. In the morning …"

Tate allowed her fingers to slip away. He leaned far over and kissed her on the forehead. She closed her eyes. And then she smiled. He saw her smile.

Like a sail, his whole being filled with the wind of God.

* * *

In the lobby, he dialed Hadashi's number—this time he remembered it without a problem—but there was still no answer. *Perhaps he's ill,* Tate thought. But he dismissed the possibility. The way he felt now, no one could be ill! *Maybe he's shut off the phone; or maybe he's away.*

Filled with energy, Tate fairly burst out of the hospital doors and charged down the walk. People stared at him—he took no notice. Without thinking, giving himself over completely to his rejoicing heart, he strode in the direction of the center of the city. He was surprised when he found himself there, on Ben-Yehuda Street; he didn't really know how he'd arrived. It was early evening; darkness had not long ago fallen. All the stores were open, the sidewalks were thronged, traffic was impossible. He passed a store that sold religious articles and glanced at it absently. Suddenly, he stopped and went back. For several moments he stared at the Hebrew prayer books and exotic-looking objects in the window display. On impulse, he entered. "Excuse me," he said. "Do you speak English?"

The storekeeper, a short, squat man wearing a black skullcap and a faded brown sweater, was alone. He nodded. "Yes, I speak English," he said in a thick accent that Tate could not identify. "Can I be of help to you?"

Tate looked around the store.

The storekeeper stared at him. After a moment, he said, "You're not Jewish. This is like … an alien planet. Is that it?"

"I'm not Jewish."

"It doesn't matter," said the storekeeper. "Don't be embarrassed or uncomfortable. Feel free to ask questions. I'll be happy to answer them, if I can."

Tates hesitated. "Is—is there a holiday now?"

"A holiday?"

"Yes. Is there a Jewish holiday here, in the country, at this time?"

The storekeeper shook his head. "No, there's no Jewish holiday now in Israel."

"Is there one coming up?"

"'Coming up?' I don't understand—"

"I mean, will be there be one soon?"

"No," said the storekeeper, "there won't be one until the spring." He adjusted his skullcap. "But we had one not so very long ago."

"Oh? Which was it?"

"Chanukah."

"Happy or sad?"

"Happy," said the storekeeper. "Very happy. Chanukah is called 'the festival of lights.' We celebrate it to remember the victory of the Maccabees over the pagan Greek conquerors. It proclaims the triumph of freedom over tyranny." The speaker smiled. "In ancient times, when it happened, there was a miracle—"

"A miracle? What miracle?"

The storekeeper ran a hand over the gray and white stubble on his cheeks and chin. "The victorious Jews wished to rekindle the *ner-tamid*—the eternal light—in the Temple, which had been defiled by the Greeks. They found oil enough only for a single day. But the lamp burned for eight consecutive days, until new oil could be brought. Today, Jews light an eight-branched Chanukah lamp to commemorate the eight days of the miracle. The lamps burn either with candles or olive-oil."

"Do you have one?"

"One what?"

"A Chanukah lamp."

The storekeeper laughed. "I have many! Here, let me show you—" He indicated a shelf to the right.

Tate pointed. "That one—"

"Which—?"

"That one—the one on the extreme left."

"With the lions?"

"Yes, that's it. With the lions."

Tate held the brass Chanukah lamp with the twin Lions of Judah facing each other close to his chest. "Have you the oil?"

The storekeeper turned. "I have the oil. And the wicks, as well." As he wrapped the items, he explained how to fill the glass cups and insert the wicks. When Tate had paid him and was about to leave, he said: "Please forgive my curiosity, but are you actually planning to light the lamp?"

"Yes."

"Now, after the holiday?"

"Yes."

"Despite the fact that—that you're not Jewish?"

Tate nodded.

"Would it be too forward of me to ask you why?"

Tate shook his head. "I, too," he said, hugging his package to him, "wish to celebrate a miracle."

"Miracle? What miracle?"

Tate tried, but could not speak. So he simply turned and left the store.

* * *

Carefully, Tate poured oil into the glass cuplets of his Chanukah lamp until all of them were filled. He was about to put the bottle down on the dresser next to the lamp when his eye caught the label. The Hebrew characters intrigued him. These were the very letters and words that Jesus had used to speak and to write: *Jesus's tongue*. He placed the bottle off to one side and, one by one, inserted the wicks. He stood back. That was it. All was ready. Just one final step—he wanted the lights off. Quickly, he moved from switch to switch and returned to the dresser.

It was then that he discovered he had no matches. He felt disappointed. The letdown was so keen that it bordered on dismay. He shook his head. "No matches! Not one single match!" he murmured to himself. He could not understand his reaction to what was obviously a minor problem. "It's silly," he told himself. "I'm behaving like a child." Still, the feeling persisted. Somehow, he was disturbed by the snag; he had wanted nothing to go amiss with the lighting of his lamp.

Of course it was easy to set things right. He could do it in the time it would take him to get down to the lobby and back up to the room. He slipped into the shirt he'd thrown off when he entered the room and, still buttoning it, hurried out the door. At the bar, he asked for a book of matches and at once received one with the name of the hotel emblazoned on its cover in gold. But he had to wait for an elevator; it seemed that every guest in the place was using them. The delay irked him. Quite unnecessarily, he thought—but he was unable to shake his impatience. He was anxious, as well. That he hadn't a match to kindle his miracle lamp—what did it mean? Was it some negative sign? A warning? He wasn't, and had never been, a superstitious man. And yet this bothered him, dug into him. Again, he rebuked himself for being childish. And then he felt sorry for himself. Why should he judge himself harshly? So what if he acted like a kid who'd discovered that his adored baseball glove was missing? After all he'd been through these last few days, who could blame him? He was entitled to be upsct and irrational.

The elevator came and he elbowed his way in. It seemed to take forever to reach his floor. Back in the dark room, he stood in front of the lamp, which he'd centered on the dresser top. He withdrew the book of matches from his pocket, struck one, and guarded it with the other hand to make certain that it didn't go out. That would have been too much. The first match had to do. He had set his mind on that, and knew that nothing would assuage him if he were to fail. He touched the burning match to the first wick. *There!* It burst gently into flame. His hand moved on, protected always by the other hand. The match must not go out. *Two—three—four* … He could not fail. *Five—six* … A single match had to light all. That was the way it was. No reason. No explanation. The way it was. *Seven—eight* … He breathed a sigh of relief. It was done. He'd succeeded. The entire lamp blazed. One frail match had borne the burden. To the left, beyond the bottle of olive oil, was an ashtray. He dropped the burned match into it. He threw the matchbook down beside it.

When the lamp was lit, he had intended to pray, but a disturbing thought came to mind. Had the storekeeper instructed him to kindle the lamp from right to left—or the reverse? *What does that matter?* he thought. But somehow it did. He wanted to have done it in the correct way; now it was done, and he'd never know. He had wanted perfection. That he might have done things wrong pricked and unsettled him. More unsettling still was the fact that trivial things bothered him. He had no right to fuss over inconsequential detail, yet he seemed incapable of dismissing it. What ailed him? What made him feel like a wobbling gyroscope?

Never once taking his eyes from the eight ruby flames and the twin Lions of Judah, their brass flanks running with ruddy light, he backed up and sat on the bed. He tried once more to pray, but couldn't seem to formulate his message. As before he'd lacked matches, now he lacked words; nothing ignited the wick of his mind. He felt utterly drained, sapped of strength. Still watching the lamp, he stretched himself out on the bed.

He didn't sleep, didn't even doze. He just lay there in the dark, mesmerized by the burning lamp and its mirror image. After a while, his tension left him. He thought of how warmly Dr. Elfenbaum had conveyed the good news to him, he remembered Margie's eyes looking up at him, he saw himself leaning over and kissing her forehead. He relaxed; he felt that he was drifting in some unsinkable skiff. He stared at the lamp. The oil in the cuplets had been soaked up. One flame flickered and went out; then another and another. Then the last one—on the far left—guttered, winked several times and finally disappeared. He felt utterly at peace. *Prayer was unnecessary. God understood without it.*

Jerusalem, December 27, 1992
Hilton Hotel
6:03 am

In the morning, he woke up and, to his surprise, found that he was wearing his pajamas—he had no memory whatsoever of getting undressed and putting them on. He reached down and switched on the radio. Bright, buoyant music spilled out. He was glad. It fitted his mood. Margie's recovery was real, and it was all right for him to revel in that fact! As he moved toward the bathroom, he noted the time on the TV clock: it was just past six. That was perfect, he thought jubilantly. He'd be able to arrive at the hospital early and spend as much time with Margie as her strength would allow.

He shaved with particular care, *the way a bridegroom shaves on the morning of his wedding day*, he thought with a smile. He brushed his teeth—vigorously, with an energy that was almost explosive. Then he stripped his pajamas off and got into the tub. He pulled the shower curtain shut with one stroke and turned the water to hot. Spray danced on his glistening skin; clouds of steam filled the room. As he dried himself, yanking every towel he could find off the rack, he hummed snatches of the "Ode to Joy." There was a good reason, he reflected, that he'd played that music in her room. He had sensed what was coming. He sprinkled himself with talc and smoothed it on. Then, standing at the sink, he patted Margie's favorite aftershave lotion over his face and neck.

Now for his attire. He picked the clothing with Margie in mind: the beautiful flannel shirt she'd given him last Christmas, pants that she'd helped him buy a couple of weeks before they came on the trip, socks that she'd brought him as a present for "no special reason at all," suede shoes that she'd admired when he came home from the mall with them. Still humming, he dressed. He stood in front of the full-length mirror and looked at himself. He was more than satisfied. Margie would be delighted; it always pleased her when he took pains with his appearance. "Alan," she'd say, "what a handsome husband!" Something like that.

Once dressed, he could give attention to the Chanukah lamp. First off, he removed and discarded the used wicks. Next, he rinsed out and dried the glass cuplets in turn. Then he got a clean handkerchief from a dresser drawer and wiped the entire brass surface of the lamp. He held it up for inspection, and when he was satisfied that there was not a speck of dust anywhere, he rewrapped it in the paper the storekeeper had used. Finally, he opened the bottom drawer of the dresser and put it in. When Margie was better, really better, he'd bring it to her. "Here," he'd say, here is your miracle lamp. I bought it for you in a store on Ben-Yehuda Street, the very first day you came out of the coma." He'd hold it up to the light so that she could see it clearly—her sight would be perfect or at least improved by then—and tell her how he'd put it on the dresser in their room and kindled it, all eight wicks, on a single match and watched it burn in celebration of her recovery. "Look here," he'd say. "These are the twin Lions of Judah. They will guard and protect you. Always and forever!" And she'd laugh and say, "Alan, what an undaunted romantic you are!" But he wasn't just a romantic; he was a realist, too. He had a keen sense of "real" life, and he had an uncanny feel for what lay behind it. She was entitled to disbelieve all she wanted; she could joke to her heart's content, but the lions would watch over her. Not literally, of course. But why even get into the philosophy? He was quite sure that she'd love and appreciate the lamp and its symbolism—and that was exactly what he wanted.

Downstairs, he did not choose the coffee shop. This morning, it seemed too skimpy, too cramped, for his mood. He went instead to the main dining room, with its drapes and chandeliers and snow-white tablecloths and heavy silverware. Why not? He was zestful; he was even hungry! Enjoying himself, he made his way along the lavishly stocked buffet table and made his choices. Smoked salmon and herring, three or four varieties of cheese, mixed salad and fruit, chilled tomato juice and coffee. He ate with the feeling that Margie was with him. *And she would be!*

Tate breathed deeply. The day was brilliant—a newly-minted coin. In the taxi, he said to the driver, "I'm going to Mt. Zion Hospital, but I'd like to buy some flowers first. Would you please take me to the nearest flower shop?"

The driver held up a wrist and tapped his watch. "Too early—"

Tate looked at his own watch. "Twenty-five after seven. I guess it is too early," he said with disappointment.

The driver turned the ignition switch. "No problem," he said. "I'll take you to the *shuk*."

It was only a short drive. Tate moved past the vegetable, fruit, and clothing stalls of the Machaneh Yehuda market until he came to a flower stand. He took his time and in the end chose roses. Long-stemmed. Saffron. He'd never seen a color like it. Handing the vendor a fifty-shekel note, he said, "They're exquisite."

The vendor shrugged. "No speak English—" He gave Tate the change. "Yiddish … Russian … Arabic?" he said with a gold-toothed smile.

The taxi driver proved to be fantastic. He took all kinds of ancillary routes and shortcuts to avoid the congested traffic. Even with the excursion to the market, they reached the hospital in what had to be record time. "You're really a terrific driver—a wizard," Tate said to the driver as he got out.

"A wiz…ard?"

"A magician."

"Ah," said the driver, "that's what my wife always says …"

Another first: Tate caught an elevator right off. It was empty, and he was up in virtually no time at all. Cradling his roses, he hurried into the ICU ward. It had a strange look about it. Something very odd. He stopped where he was. *Margie's bed was empty!* That's what it was! A hand touched his shoulder. He turned. "Tova," he said, "what's going on around here? Where's Margie? Why isn't she in her bed?"

The nurse's heavy face looked almost sullen. "Dr. Katz will speak with you. He's over at the nurses' station."

"But where is Margie? Why is her bed empty?" He held up the roses. "See, I have flowers for her. Aren't they something?"

"Please, Mr. Tate. Dr. Katz will speak with you—"

It seemed to take him more time to get to the nurses' station than it had taken to get to the hospital. A lanky man with gold-rimmed glasses and wispy, brown hair wearing an ill-fitting white coat extended a hand.

Tate ignored it. "My wife—"

"I'm Dr. Katz, Mr. Tate. I'm the intern on duty. Why don't we step out into the corridor for a moment so we can talk more comfortably?"

Tate followed the white coat.

Dr. Katz halted and turned. "Mr. Tate," he said slowly, "your wife … is presently undergoing surgery—"

"Surgery? What are you talking about?"

"She went into the operating theater about twenty minutes ago."

"Why wasn't I informed?"

"We called the hotel," said Katz, "but we couldn't get hold of you—"

Tate cut him off. "But why is she in surgery? She was out of the coma. She was getting well—"

"Early this morning, Mrs. Tate's situation changed radically. Her condition began to deteriorate. I contacted Dr. Elfenbaum immediately. He examined her, and decided that it was necessary to put in a shunt—"

Tate shook his head. "You don't understand, Dr. Katz. Yesterday, I spoke to her. She spoke to me. She was awake. She even smiled. She was getting better." He held up the flowers. "See, I've brought roses for her. The color's exquisite, no?"

Dr. Katz said nothing. It seemed that he might reach out and touch Tate, but after a moment he reached up and adjusted his glasses. "I just want you to know ... that we're doing everything we can. And I'd like to add personally that Dr. Elfenbaum is the very best." Katz cleared his throat. "We'll keep you posted, Mr. Tate."

"She was getting well. Margie was getting well ..."

Tate sat on one of the chairs in the alcove down at the end of the corridor, the roses on his lap. Tova came to visit him several times, but he paid no attention to her. She spoke to him, but he only shook his head. "You don't understand—"

The hospital clock said ten to twelve. Round face. Polished glass. Thick black hour hand. Thick black minute hand. Thin red second hand, jerking forward. *'Signifying nothing,'* he thought. Then he thought nothing.

He came alive again when he heard the footsteps. Knew whose they were before he saw the man. Knew what the man would say before he said it. Did not look up until the man stood directly in front of him, practically touching him.

"Mr. Tate—Alan—"

He raised his eyes. Dr. Elfenbaum looked old. He wasn't much more than fifty, but the oldness had come out in him. He said three words: "We've lost her ..." There was a pause and he said two more: "I'm sorry—"

The saffron roses fell to the floor.

Jerusalem, December 27, 1992
Mt. Zion Hospital
1:12 pm

Tate stood outside the hospital. People passed him. An unending parade of people. He paid them no heed. He just stood there on the concrete walk, staring into the bright afternoon sunshine. After a time, he turned and walked stiffly back to where the taxis waited in line. He got into the first one. "To the Old City," he said to the driver.

The taxi started. Cars passed him. An unending parade of cars. He paid them no heed. The driver spoke. To Tate, his words were like leaves, wet autumn leaves dumped from a wheelbarrow after they'd been raked up. *Let them rot where they lay!* The driver kept on yammering. Finally, Tate made out that he was asking a question. "Where to in the Old City?"

That required an answer. "Jaffa gate," he said.

"Jaffa gate?"

"Yes," said Tate. "My wife's waiting for me there."

Of course, it turned out that she wasn't. He'd known that she wouldn't be there all the time. Still, it had been worth the try. What if on some off chance, she appeared? You could never tell for sure. Stranger things had happened in the history of the world. The taxi disappeared into traffic. He'd watched it go, for no apparent reason—just watched it go. He stood outside the Jaffa gate. For the same nonreason. People passed him by. An unending stream. They, too, disappeared. Into the traffic of people. He stood there on the sidewalk, staring into the bright afternoon sunlight. What was next?

The museum. The Tower of David Museum. Of course. He went through the gate and swerved to the right and entered the museum structure that incorporated the Old City wall. He walked swiftly up to the ticket booth. "How much?"

"Fourteen shekels," said the ticket seller.

When Tate reached into his pocket to get the money, a piece of paper fell out. He paid it no heed. A man standing behind him bent down and retrieved it. "Here, mister. You dropped this—"

Tate took it. Stared at it. There were names. Telephone numbers. Addresses. He remembered fragmentarily: hospital personnel, government officials, American Embassy, death certificate, flight arrangements, burial—all given to him at the hospital. But the scribbled words were like sparks;

they went shooting up the chimney of his mind and out. As quickly as he'd remembered, he dismissed the memories.

"Another shekel, please," said the ticket seller: "You're short one—"

"Ah, yes …" Tate handed over the last shekel. He stuffed the scrap of paper with the names and numbers and addresses back in his pocket. He took the ticket. "My wife's waiting for me inside …"

She wasn't, of course. He looked for her everywhere, visiting all the exhibits the two of them had seen together. He did a remarkably thorough job. That was his nature. She did not turn up. Still, he wouldn't quit. That was his nature. The museum was extensive: there were dozens of exhibits, inside and out in the open. He might not have seen her; might have missed her in his very eagerness. They could easily have passed each other by. That happened sometimes. Everything happened sometimes. *Something had happened to him. He didn't know what.*

A voice spoke to him. Well, that happened too. You could ignore it for just so long. Then you had to address it. That was the rule. The world was made up of rules; that was a rule in and of itself. The category of categories. Something like that. The voice was still going. He turned and saw a man in uniform. "Am I under arrest?" Tate asked.

"Pardon me?"

"I'll go quietly," said Tate. "I won't make any fuss." Expecting to be cuffed, he held out his hands. "But I wish you to know that I don't understand the charges. Someone will have to explain them to me. The judge. Or the bailiff. Or the prosecuting attorney. Or maybe the jury—to tell you the truth, I've forgotten which. In the end, they all get mixed up together anyway—"

"It's closing time, sir."

"You're speaking English," said Tate. "That's good, because I don't speak Hebrew. Jesus spoke Hebrew. But I'm not Jesus. I'm sorry …"

"The museum is closing shortly, sir. You'll have to leave."

Tate nodded. To leave. Everybody had to leave everywhere. The world was built on leaving. "I'll be going now," Tate said. "Thank you."

*   *   *

He stood outside the museum. It was already dark. He walked to Jaffa gate and through it to the thoroughfare beyond the Old City wall and hailed a passing cab.

"Where do you want to go?" said the driver.

He had to think about it.

"Sir?"

"Give me time—"

"I can't just stand here, sir. I'll have to start the meter."

"Start it."

His thoughts led him nowhere. They were tangled, like wool escaped from a skein. Then—out of the blue—it came to him. "Take me to Independence Park."

The driver threw the car into gear. "To Independence Park—correct?"

"Yes. My wife's waiting for me there."

Even though it was dark, he found the bench. The same one they'd sat on together. What a lovely word, *together*! People ought to use it more often. He stared at the empty bench. He'd found it all right, but Margie wasn't there. He looked at his watch. Couldn't make out the time, but it didn't matter. He had arrived too early. That was the problem. He was too early and he'd have to wait for her. Sit himself down and wait patiently. That was all. It was simple. So many things were really simple if people let them be … .

He sat on the bench. Occasionally, someone passed. He couldn't make out who—it was much too dark. All he could see were shadows. But what if … one of the passing shadows was Margie? He became alarmed. He felt he had to call out. Call her name so that she'd know he was there, waiting patiently for her on the bench. "*Margie!*" His voice sounded hollow, wispy, insubstantial. It was silly. He was wrong. Margie wouldn't just go past him: she had promised to come over and sit next to him and hold his hand. *To hold her hand: that was all he wanted* …

Shadows passed. Dragged by. Flitted by. Sprung of darkness, they melted into darkness. Mostly couples: he heard their intertwined voices. They whispered. Laughed. Conspired. The single shadows were men—he could tell by the determined heaviness of their steps. One of them came by whistling. Some nameless tune that was painful to hear; the notes struck Tate's ears like porcupine quills. Then the song faded and was erased—as if it had never been at all. And then there was silence. And more passing shadows. A line popped into Tate's mind:

" … *That Shadow entering human graves* …"

Where had he read it? In some poem, long ago. He struggled to recall, but at each attempt his mind struck a reef. Tate watched his thoughts go down like ships. Men were so afraid of thoughts. Because they were seldom pure. Because they were mostly feeling. Thoughts were but the tip of an iceberg. The rest, what lay beneath the surface, was feeling. Thoughts shot out of a man's mind like bullets. *Bang! Bang! Bang!* Watch them hit their mark! *Bang!* You're dead! Felled by a single thought to the head!

It got colder. His body told him, not his mind. His teeth began to chatter. He shook. The temperature had really dropped. Mountain-top Jerusalem shivered with him. Maybe Margie hadn't told him that she'd meet him in the park after all? Maybe he'd made a mistake? Maybe he'd misunderstood her? It was terrible. Lately, he was always misunderstanding her. He rose from the bench. The park was deserted. An empty tomb. Someone had stolen the body.

* * *

This time, he walked. To hell with taxis! The drivers talked too much. Hands in his pockets, head lowered, he walked. He was a bull, charging through the night. When he raised his eyes, he was at the corner of Jaffa Road and King George Street. Ah, yes, that was the corner. Then where was the restaurant? He looked around. There it was! On the other side. He'd completely mixed up the direction. But now it had all come right. He crossed over, nearly being hit by a car. The driver honked and shouted out the window. Why? So Tate had crossed against the light, what the devil did it matter? What good were lights? What could they stop? Disease? Death?

Fefferberg's was quite crowded. The proprietor, a short man wearing rumpled, black trousers, a white shirt, and brown suspenders, approached. "My wife is waiting for me," Tate explained. "I got confused. It happens sometimes. I thought I was to meet her in the park, but actually she's here. Would you tell her I've arrived, please?"

The proprietor looked puzzled. "Your wife? What does she look like?"

"She's, well—oh, never mind," said Tate impatiently. "I'll find her myself." He roamed through the restaurant. At length, he turned. "It seems she's not." The other man followed him. *Quite like a hound*, Tate thought, as he here," said Tate. "She's probably on her way."

"Would you care to sit down and wait?"

Tate nodded. "Yes, yes. That would be fine."

There was a table in the rear. A secluded table for two. Margie liked to look out, so he took the seat facing the wall. He waited expectantly, playing with his silverware. To his right were a glass ashtray and a white vase with a single red carnation. He waved to the waiter. "Remove this, please," he said, pointing a finger.

The waiter reached for the ashtray.

"No, no," he snapped: "Not the ashtray—the flower. I hate flowers!"

But he did not know why.

All around him, people ate. Shoved forks and spoons into their mouths. Chewed. Swallowed. Swilled. Swept napkins across their lips. It made no sense to him; he was watching some meaningless spectacle. The waiter appeared. "Would you care for something to drink, sir? While you're waiting? Some wine? A glass of beer, perhaps?"

"Nothing."

Gradually, the restaurant emptied. One by one, the tables were deserted. Tate heard the chairs scraping back. The exchanges of greeting. Every time the door creaked on its hinges, he turned around to look for Margie. Every time he looked, it was only customers leaving. He saw stained and littered tablecloths and at the very front an old man, slurping coffee from a saucer. Then the old man was gone.

"Sir—"

"Eh?"

It was the damn waiter again. "Sir, we're about to close the kitchen."

"But my wife is on her way over here."

"I'm very sorry, sir, but we close at this hour."

"What hour?"

"Eleven o'clock, sir."

"Why do you close at eleven? What's so damn special about eleven? Why not twelve? Or, better still, one?"

The waiter brought the proprietor, who frowned. "Sir—"

Tate cut him off. "Don't 'sir' me. You don't seem to understand. My wife is coming. She wasn't in the museum and she wasn't in the park, so it stands to reason that she's coming here. We're going to have dinner." He waved a hand. "We were here the other day and we had a splendid meal." He tapped his forehead. "But I don't recall exactly what we ordered. Do you?"

The proprietor's face looked dark, as if a cloud had come over it.

"Is something wrong?" Tate asked.

"We're closing up now, sir. We won't be able to serve you this evening. Why don't you and your wife come in tomorrow?"

"Tomorrow," said Tate. "When is that?"

* * *

The Shrine of the Book! It was obvious! Why hadn't he thought of it before? That's where Margie was sure to be! She'd told him explicitly that she wanted to see the National Museum and the Shrine of the Book again, so it was clear that she'd gone there. He struck his forehead with the heel of his hand. What in the world was wrong with him these days? He forgot the things he should have remembered, and remembered the things he should have forgotten.

But when he told the taxi driver where he wanted to go, the man looked at him strangely. "Now? You want to go there now?"

"My wife is there. She's waiting for me. She told me that she wanted to go back there again—and I forgot completely. I don't know what's gotten into me—"

"But it's nearly midnight. Those places aren't open."

"Not open?"

The driver shook his head. "No, they're not," he said emphatically: "Maybe I can take you somewhere else?"

"Where?" said Tate.

*　　*　　*

He was walking. Walking, walking, walking. Now he was sorry he hadn't taken that blasted taxi, because his legs were like lead. Like slabs of marble. *His body*. Always his body. He had to drag it around after him like a millstone, bumping and scraping over the pavement. He had to lug his body around with him like a dung beetle with its load. He kept walking. The taxi driver said he would have taken him "somewhere else." Tate had made a big mistake: he should have gone "somewhere else" with that driver. It was too late now. He couldn't seem to get a cab, no matter how hard he tried. The ones that slipped by—and they were infrequent—carried passengers. Either passengers or store dummies. Or shadows. It was all the same to him. He was condemned to walk, so he walked. Pushed his legs, pulled his carcass. Heavy as granite. Only his mind floated. Soared. Zoomed right up to the stratosphere like a helium balloon gone wild. Above it all. Free and unfettered. Wasn't that what minds were for?

He stopped. This wouldn't do. Simply would not do. Walking and walking and never getting there. If he kept walking through the night, he would run smack into the day. But he didn't have the strength to face the day. Not yet. Perhaps never. He looked around. All the windows in all the houses and buildings were dark. The stone was asleep. The city was shut down. Perhaps the world was shut down as well?

Above him, a street lamp flickered. He had no idea where he was. Heaven? Hell? Paradise? Purgatory? He was a stranger in all of them, anyway. He shivered. He had no idea of how he'd gotten there, either. Had his legs done this to him? Why? What had he ever done to them? A car came creeping along the street. He stepped off the curb. This was his big chance. "Taxi—"

With an arm dangling on the door and the other resting on the steering wheel, the driver looked up at him. The man had a crude-featured, grizzled face and thick lips; he wore some kind of a uniform.

"You're not a taxi," said Tate.

The man smiled tolerantly. "We're the police."

"I'm lost," said Tate.

"You're a tourist?"

"I'm visiting. With my wife. She was supposed to meet me in the restaurant, but she never showed up. I was looking for her. Then I got lost."

"I see," said the policeman. "Where do you stay?"

"At the hotel."

"Which hotel?"

Tate thought. "How ridiculous of me," he said after a moment. "I've forgotten the name. I keep forgetting things these days. Does it ever happen to you?"

"May I have a look at your ID, sir?"

Tate groped in the inner pocket of his jacket. No, not the book of travelers' checks. The passport. He handed it over to the policeman.

"American, eh?"

Tate said nothing. He waited and then took the passport back.

The driver's partner leaned over. "Can you tell us something about where your hotel is located? Could you describe it, please?"

Tate thought. The balloon came down. Not all the way down. But down, nevertheless. "It's a tower," he said, "on a hill. You can see the whole city from it. And there's a big auditorium next door. They seem to have all kinds of exhibitions there, though my wife and I have never gone in. Oh, yes, and the bus station's not far away …"

"The Hilton," said the first policeman.

"Ah, the Hilton," said Tate: "I should have known that! How silly of me! Margie'll have a good laugh—"

"Please," said the other policeman, "come into the car. We'll give you a lift."

Tate needed one.

* * *

In the lobby, he found a table not far from the bar and seated himself. Twice, the waitress came over and asked him if he wanted anything. Twice, he told her that he didn't. "I'm waiting for my wife," he said. "We're going to have a drink together. She should be here soon."

It was past two. He glanced around. In the entire lobby, there were only seven guests: three nattily dressed South American businessmen (he could always spot businessmen from a mile off) whose Spanish crackled crisply all the way to where Tate sat; a sleek Oriental couple—he in a dark, pin-striped suit and she in a tight-fitting, slit-skirted dress imprinted with gold, red, and purple bird-of-paradise flowers; and an elderly English gentleman who looked as if he had been embalmed. The South Americans left first; then the Englishman rose stiffly and departed; last to go were the Orientals, holding each other's waists and pretending to kiss. For the third time, the waitress approached. She wore her red hair short and her skirt shorter. "Are you sure you wouldn't like something, sir?"

Tate considered. Maybe the waitress had a point. Margie might be late; something might have delayed her. It really wouldn't hurt if he had a drink before she joined him. "Do you have brandy?" he asked.

"Yes, sir, we certainly do. Any particular kind? We have a very fine Israeli brandy. I'm sure you'll like it."

"Yes," Tate agreed. "I'll like it. I know I'll like it."

The waitress brought the brandy and Tate drank it. Before she'd taken ten steps, he waved a hand. "Miss—" She returned. "Another one, please," he said.

He had four. Then, quite suddenly, it seemed to him, the waitress appeared on her own. That was fine, because he wanted to order a fifth. He was very cold; the brandy warmed him. But before he had a chance to tell her, she said, "We're closing up now, sir."

"Excuse me?"

"The bar is closed."

"But my wife is coming. We're going to have a drink together."

The waitress had an odd expression on her face. "Good night, sir."

With the exception of the doorman, who was yammering with the bell captain, and the lone clerk at the reception desk, the lobby was empty. Everyone else had flown the coop. He was alone, the last candle.

It was time to extinguish himself.

* * *

The doorknob was there, just in front of him. It seemed to gleam, like some malevolent planet that had broken loose from its orbit. It was simple. He had to take the key out of his pocket, insert it in the keyhole, turn and remove it; then he had to take hold of the knob and open the door. That would settle everything. The ordeal would be over. Finished for good. He would enter the room and find Margie there. Waiting for him. They would embrace each other, laugh about having missed each other so many times, fall upon the bed in each other's arms and make love. Just as they always had; just as they always would. Then they'd sleep, their bodies touching, their dreams intertwined. All else was a mistake. A misunderstanding. A medley of bungled cues and false directions. She had told him that she was staying in the room and he had completely misinterpreted what she said. It was so clear, so patent, so logical. It explained everything. Why hadn't he thought of the room before? It had taken four Israeli brandies to jog his memory.

He went into the room and quietly closed the door behind him. The curtain was drawn over the terrace window; he was in total darkness. "Margie?"

The silence slapped his face.

But then he shook his head. Of course! How asinine could he get? He chuckled to himself. It was after three in the morning. She was asleep. Why shouldn't she be asleep? They'd had a busy day. They'd talk in the morning. Make love when they woke up. Clumsily, falling all over himself, he undressed. Got into bed with extreme care, so as not to disturb her. Crawled under the blanket and gently pulled it up. He smiled. How he had missed her! *How good it was to be with her again!*

Jerusalem, December 28, 1992
Hilton Hotel
7:28 am

The noise was terrible.

It rubbed his mind like sandpaper. He didn't even open his eyes—he just kept them shut and wished the noise would go away. It didn't. What the devil was it? Then he realized the phone was ringing. With his eyelids still glued together, he reached out and picked up the receiver. "Hello," he said hoarsely. "Who is it?"

The voice on the line spat at him; it grated on his ears like a broken soundtrack. He could not seem to separate the sentences one from the other or disentangle the ideas. "American Embassy … Israeli authorities … Mt. Zion Hospital … flight arrangements for the body … forms to fill out … instructions for shipping—" He had trouble unscrambling the words. "Mr. Tate? Are you there, Mr. Tate?"

Mr. Tate? Well, he was Mr. Tate. That was established. Was he there? He sure was. That couldn't be disputed. But there was one more thing he had heard. There it was again: " … *the late Mrs. Tate* …" He sat up. He turned his head. Sunlight surged against the drawn curtain like water straining to burst a dike. Margie's place was empty; she wasn't there.

"Mr. Tate? Hello. Are you there?"

"No," he whispered and hung up.

* * *

The phone kept ringing. He ignored it, but that didn't stop it. Finally, he lifted the receiver and left it off the hook. Staring at the empty place in the bed, he stared at the truth. Margie wasn't there. He had to face it. Squarely. Without retreat. She was gone. He had to confront it. Coldly. Surgically. Inescapably. She was gone and she wasn't coming back. He had to record that fact. To computerize it. There was no sidestepping, no avoiding, no denying. *She had gone—and he would go too.*

He got out of bed. Stripped off the clothes he'd fallen asleep in. Threw them to the floor. They were, after all, the clothes he'd picked for a wedding; he couldn't very well use them for a funeral. Then he went into the bathroom. Shaved. Showered. Came out clean. Dried himself off. Didn't use any aftershave lotion: there was absolutely no need for it. Went back into the other room. Opened the closet. Put on fresh clothes: didn't pick them, just took what came to hand. Made certain he had everything: travelers' checks, passport, wallet, small change, key.

Then he went after her purse. Where had he placed it? In the top drawer of the dresser, over on the right. Found it right off. Held it in both hands and stared at it. Coldly. With detachment. As one would stare at "Exhibit A" in the courtroom. There were faded spots of blood all over it: her blood. But it was nothing to dwell on; she certainly didn't need blood now.

He unzipped the purse and dumped its contents onto the dresser. Methodically, with no more than clinical interest, he sorted through what was there: tortoise-shell comb and matching pocket mirror, which he'd given her as a gift many years ago (he remembered the store and even the clerk who'd waited on him); lipstick; packet of Kleenex; silver and black pen—he'd given her that as well, on a birthday; checkbook (she'd always kept the household accounts); ring of keys; ornate sterling silver box that had belonged to her mother's mother, in which she kept pills; passport; and money in a small leather wallet on which her initials, "M. T.," were stamped in gold that had begun to peel. There was also a leather change purse that clinked as he took it out. He thrust a hand inside the purse and emptied it of coins.

He kept only the passport, the pen, and the wallet. The rest he swept into the wastebasket. The purse itself followed. That was that. Stage One. He had completed it.

* * *

Downstairs, in the lobby, he spotted the young reception clerk from Paris behind the desk. As Tate approached, the clerk smiled his anything-to-please smile. No names, Tate knew, had appeared in the media reports of the stoning incident; only that the police were searching for the Arab who'd done it. A passerby had caught sight of him. Tate would be left alone. Spared the prying and the meddling of strangers, well meaning as they might be. Free to execute the stages of his plan. "Good morning," the clerk said.

"Good morning," replied Tate. Stay calm. Focus on Stage Two. That was the ticket.

"Mrs. Tate sleeping late?" asked the clerk.

Tate turned his head. Calm. Steady. Icy, if need be. He faced around again. "Would you have a copy of the *Yellow Pages*?" he asked.

"I'm sure we do. Just one moment, please."

"I'll wait."

The clerk returned with the grin of a conqueror. "Here you are, Mr. Tate. The *Jerusalem Yellow Pages*."

"Thanks. I'll bring it back when I'm finished."

In a seat by the window, all the way across the lobby from the desk, Tate did not find what he wanted under "G." He looked under "W." There were two weapons stores listed; he wrote the names and addresses down on a cocktail napkin. He used Margie's pen, the black and silver one. It was fitting, he thought.

When he brought the *Yellow Pages* back, the clerk looked disturbed. His hoping-to-help smile had been replaced by a nervous something's-terribly-wrong one. "Mr. Tate—"

"I've finished. Here's the book."

"Mr. Tate, the American Embassy has been trying to reach you. They say it's urgent. And there are other messages as well—all of them urgent. Mr. Tate? Did you hear me? Mr. Tate?"

But Tate was gone. So was Stage Two.

* * *

The proprietor was short, egg-bald, with a smooth-skinned, cupidlike face and a thick, black mustache. He shook his head. "No, no," he said. "I'm sorry, but I can't sell you a rifle without a permit." He stared at his customer. "You don't have a permit, do you?"

Tate shook his head. "Where do I get one?"

"The police. You must apply to the police for a permit."

"What will they want to know?"

The proprietor fidgeted. "They'll want to know what you want a rifle for. Why you need it. For instance, if you live in a dangerous area, like the *sh'tachim*—the West Bank, that is, or near Gaza."

Tate shrugged. "But the rifle's a gift for my son. A birthday present."

"You're a tourist?"

"A visitor."

"Perhaps I can have it sent directly from the store to the airport." The proprietor scratched an ear. "You could pick it up at customs there. When you leave. I'm not sure, though. I'll have to check. If you'll be kind enough to leave your telephone number—"

Tate shook his head. "That's no good. No good at all. My son's birthday is tomorrow. We're having a party for him at the hotel. I want to give it to him then. Surprise him …"

"I'd like to accommodate you," said the proprietor, "but I'm afraid it's impossible."

"No permit, no rifle. And that's final?"

"That's it."

"No way around it?"

The proprietor's eyes narrowed. "What do you mean?"

Tate did not answer. Instead, he pulled out Margie's leather wallet. It was fitting, he thought. One by one, he extracted five crisp, spanking-new one hundred dollar bills. They had planned to buy something really nice for the house. Something from Israel. A painting, perhaps. Or a piece of sculpture. Margie loved sculpture; she had done a little of it herself some years back, after Sarah's death. Slowly, as if he were showing a hand in a card game, Tate spread the bills out on the counter. "Nothing will induce you to change your mind?" he asked with a smile.

The proprietor's face was chalk white. "What is this?"

"How about a pistol?" said Tate. "If I can't have a rifle, then what about a pistol?"

"Who are you?"

Tate slid the bills forward slightly. "I'd prefer an automatic."

"Sir—"

"If it's a question of another bill or two—"

"Sir, I am not allowed by law to sell you any firearm whatsoever without a permit issued by the police. I thought I'd made that perfectly clear."

Tate swept the bills up. "You'll regret it," he said.

"What's that?"

"I said that you'll regret it!" Tate stuffed the bills into his pocket and headed for the door.

"Sir!" the proprietor shouted after him. "Sir, you left a hundred-dollar bill behind—"

But Tate was gone.

The proprietor hurried to his phone and dialed the police.

* * *

He found the camping goods store halfway down Hillel Street. It had everything an outdoorsman could want or dream of: tents, kayaks, hiking boots, lanterns, cookstoves, compasses, flashlights, fishing gear—the works. It had knives, too. An entire array of them, under glass. Under lock and key. The clerk was a young woman—about as old as Sarah would have been had she lived—pretty in a kind of saucy way, with big brown eyes and blonde hair cut short with razor-sharp finesse. She put her pretty, delicate hands on the counter. "I'm looking for a knife," Tate told her.

"What kind, please?"

"A hunting knife," said Tate. "A good, solid, sturdy one. One that can really do its job." He smiled. He thought that a smile was required. He had learned from the gun store experience; he had to be cagey. Cunning. Deceptive. *The way the world was.* "It's a present," he went on, "for my son. It's his birthday. He loves the outdoors: camping, fishing, hiking—"

"I love camping myself," said the clerk with enthusiasm Tate knew was sincere. "I go on trips as often as I can."

"I see," said Tate. "My daughter was killed on a camping trip." He lifted a hand as if to fend something off. "She and her fiancé were driving ... there was ... an accident. Her name was Sarah."

"What!?"

"Nothing," said Tate quickly. "Not a thing. May I see the knives?"

"I'll show you some," said the clerk. She took a ring of keys from the shelf and bent to unlock the case. Tate saw down into her sweater: she was bra-less. Her firm, young breasts with their dark nipples reminded him of Margie's, when the two of them were living on her family's farm in Ohio. But he snapped the thread of memory at once. He erased the slate and would keep it blank. There was no place for memories now. "These are some of the best—" the clerk was saying.

There were five. Resting on the glass. At his fingertips. Tate picked up each one in turn, examining it carefully, weighing it in his hand, getting the feel of it. He narrowed the field to two and then discarded one. He held up his choice. "How about this one? It looks pretty sturdy to me." He laughed. "Someone could kill a bear with it, no?"

"It's a fine knife," nodded the clerk, "imported from England. I think it's a wise choice."

"Then I'll take it."

"Would you like me to wrap it?"

"What for?"

The pretty, young lips parted in a tolerant smile. "For your son. The birthday—"

"Ah, yes," said Tate. "Wrap it. By all means!"

The knife—with handle molded to the grip and ten-inch blade of surgical steel—came with a tooled leather sheath. The pretty clerk wrapped both in pretty paper and then affixed a bow and a sticker with the name of the store. She held forth her handiwork for the customer's inspection. "Lovely," said Tate. "Really nice. I thank you." The package went into a shopping bag, which he took from her hands.

As he went out the door, she called after him, "Tell your son happy birthday for me!"

"I certainly will," said Tate, satisfied that Stage Three had been completed.

* * *

In the washroom of a charming little restaurant up on Hanevi'im Street, he ripped the gift-wrapped package open and then fastened the sheathed knife to his belt. He buttoned his sports jacket, patted and smoothed it flat. There was a mirror over the sink and he was able to see his entire torso when he stood back. He looked fine—no one would ever guess what he had in his mind. Just before he unlocked the door, he spoke the words. Softly enough so that nobody outside could hear them, loudly enough so that he could:

> *"Blessed be the Lord, my rock*
> *Who trains my hands for war,*
> *and my fingers for battle ..."*

He was crossing the courtyard where people dined out in the summer when the waiter came running. "Sir," he called. "Excuse me, sir, but you forgot to pay for the coffee you ordered."

Tate went calmly back into the restaurant. He put a hundred-dollar bill on the counter and left.

* * *

He was on the Number 1 bus, sitting in the rear where he felt he'd be least conspicuous, when the dream suddenly came back to him. It was the dream he had the night of the day that Margie died. A simple dream. A-B-C. No convolutions. No frills. Straight to the point. He had been at the *Kotel*, and he walked from there up to the Great Mosque, the one with the five-and-dime gold roof that had turned Margie off. At the entrance, the custodian stopped him. "Sir, you must remove your shoes now."

"Take off my shoes?"

"Yes, sir."

"Why should I do a thing like that?"

"Because, sir, you will tread on holy ground."

"Yeah," he said. "Very holy, I'm sure ..."

So he took off his shoes—the suede ones that Margie liked so much—and set them along with the others and entered the mosque. The place was jam-packed, loaded to the gills, absolutely stuffed with a regular wall-to-wall circus crowd of Arabs in traditional headgear and getup. He stood for a moment, digging the scene. But he hadn't come to gawk; he was there to do a job. With a well-rehearsed flick of the wrist, he opened his trench coat, whipped out the M-16, and began firing. From the hip. Successive bursts. Point-blank. *Da-da-da-da-da-da-da!* The object being to pop as many Arabs as he could in as short a time as possible. Swing the gun. Let 'er rip. *Da-da-da-da-da-da-da!* Wipe them out. Just like a computer game. Oops! The damn magazine had run dry.

He tossed it aside. Shoved a hand into his coat pocket, where a fresh one was waiting. Yanked it out. Whacked it into place. Leveled the muzzle. Squeezed the trigger. Right to left. Left to right. No discrimination. A bullet for everyone; that was his motto. One for you. And one for you. A ticket to Allah. Free for nothing. Compliments of Tate. He sang a little ditty. To help his aim—though he didn't need to aim:

"M-16 on a dead man's chest—
Yo-ho-ho,
And a bottle of rum ..."

Now, where had he heard that? Why did it matter? As long as they went down. Like bowling pins. *Da-da-da-da-da-da-da!* Hah, they were falling like ripe apples! Like flies. Like camel turds. The wounded screamed and flailed the air. The dead said nothing; they never had anything to say—

"M-16 on a—"

Some were running. Gridlocking the exits. Piling up on each other. Trampling one another under foot. The ones who wanted to defer their interview with Allah. The ones who weren't so keen on Plastic Paradise. Well, he'd get them too. *Shit!* The blasted magazine. He'd have to reload again—

As he worked on the third clip, the voice came onto the PA system, the very same system over which the Imams called for holy war against the infidel. The voice caught his attention. Caught his heart. A song from childhood. How he'd loved it! How he loved it:

"He always sings
He always sings
A raggedy music to his cattle,
As he sways
As he sways
Back and forth on his saddle;

On a horse
On a horse
He's a syncopated gaiter,
And it's such a funny meter
To the sound of his repeater;
How they run
How they run
When they hear that fellow's gun,
All the western folks do know:
He's a high-falootin'
Rootin'-tootin'
Sonafagun from Ari-zona—
Oh, you cowboy
Ragtime cowboy
Oh, you cowboy,
Joe!"

There were tears in his eyes. Real tears—no synthetic stuff. Why, he hadn't heard that song in forty years—maybe fifty. How had the dj ever dug up the record? He never realized that anyone had made the record. Yet he'd heard it with his own ears, booming out over the hail of bullets into the big basin of the mosque. Louder than the shrieks of the dying. *Must be an ancient '78*, he thought. *A Golden Oldy. A collector's item. I'd like to send away for it. I reckon I've saved enough box tops …*

He wondered who the vocalist was. The singer, that is. Who in the name of heaven had recorded it? He didn't have the foggiest. Couldn't even say properly whether it was man or woman. It might have been Leadbelly or Perry Como or Tiny Tim or Bette Midler. Or Mahalia Jackson or Little Bo Peep or Frankie-boy. Or even Cowboy Joe himself, though that was unlikely. He had no time to solve the riddle. He had to keep firing. To keep dropping them like tin ducks at a carnival. To his surprise, he no longer had to reload. He now had free rein, total dominion. He just blasted away. *Da-da-da-da-da-da-da!* He had worked up a sweat. Hey, ventilating desert mice wasn't all that easy, you know! It was better exercise than jogging, though, any old day. What a gas! He had to laugh. *But instead, he howled.*

* * *

How had he come to have his handkerchief out? It was a mystery. But at least he knew *why* he had it out. Quickly, he dabbed his eyes. He didn't want the other bus passengers to notice. Didn't want to attract attention. He shoved the handkerchief back into a pocket. Nonchalantly, he glanced out the window. They were driving through Meah She'arim. Another fragment of the dream came back—

He was not alone in the great Disneyland mosque. No, he had a companion. A compadre. A sidekick. Tall. Slim. Muscular. Bronze-skinned. Wearing loincloth and bear-claw necklace. And on his shaven skull, not a bonnet of eagle feathers, *but a crown of thorns!* Tate snorted. "So you finally got here," he called out. "Did you come down from Bethlehem? From Nazareth? Or did you walk up from the *Kotel*?" He glanced at the newcomer. The other man looked bewildered; in frustration, he held up his Uzi.

"Hell's bells!" shouted Tate above the din. "You didn't release the safety catch! Here, let me show you—"

The newcomer nodded in appreciation as Tate took the gun and adjusted the safety catch and handed it back. "What took you so long to come?" asked Tate.

But his partner didn't answer; he was too busy shooting.

* * *

Tate got off the bus on Salah-ed-din Street. Just in front of the Dung Gate. Or was it the Lion's Gate? What did it matter? As long as he was there. He looked around. Everything seemed the same. The walls. The crowds. The cars. He stood on the sidewalk. Waited for the light. It was red. It would change to green. From red to green; from green to red; that was the way of the world. Alive one minute, dead the next. Oops, the light had turned. He crossed with the pack. Just as he had with Margie. Reached the other side. Just as he had with Margie. That was the way it had to be. The same route; exactly the same route. Just about here, she'd told him that she wanted to go back to the Tower of David Museum. He'd agreed. The same route: his own, private *via dolorosa*—

Now, he was almost there. Almost at the spot. It wouldn't take much more. Thirty—perhaps forty—feet. He had to keep calm. Cool. Steady. Collected. Nothing must arouse suspicion; nothing must interfere. "Almost, Margie—" he murmured under his breath. He saw the spot. Knew it. Would never forget it. Ten more steps—perhaps fifteen. An Arab was there. Standing motionless, gazing into traffic. He wore a red and white checked *kaffiah* and a dirty saffron robe. *Saffron*! He had a faint scar over one eye and a black mustache the size of a hair brush. Tate unfastened the button: his coat swung open. The sheath with the knife in it lay flat against his thigh. "Easy, Margie," he muttered, "easy does it." His hand grazed the handle. The knife was free—

*   *   *

He was high, so very high. Below him, so very far below him, Earth was a fly speck. He was light, so very light, as light as the ghost of a feather, and he glimpsed Earth beneath him like a mote of dust about to blow off. Then he dived. And it altered as he dropped. He was no longer light: he gained density as he streaked downward. Now, the Earth was a golf ball, an orange, a yet unripened grapefruit. He zoomed, becoming harder every second. Flint. Down he zoomed. Granite. Down. Iron. Earth was a basketball, and then a medicine ball. He was steel. Roaring down, he dipped through Earth's moody vapors—"shrouds," he called them acidly in his mind—and emerged newborn, washed in the blood of the lamb. He saw the rind of Earth, bitter as its core, the curve of its horizons, the stealthy shapes of continents. Sunlight flashed along his steel spine. He was over the shoe box of the Mediterranean. Down he raced. He was over Israel. His cutting edge spat sun-fire. Jerusalem. Salah-ed-din Street. The spot. He was one with the knife. "Now, Margie!" he screamed. He drove for the Arab's jugular—

Strong arms grabbed him. A fist smashed into his face. He blacked out.

Jerusalem, December 28, 1992
Central Police Station
3:45 pm

The room was large, plain, painted in a light green that had begun to peel. It needed a fresh coat, Tate thought. Half of one wall was a window. But not really a window: a one-way mirror. He knew that, knew it at a glance. They could try their hardest, but they couldn't fool Tate. Behind the mirror were the mucky-mucks. Watching every move; listening to every sound. Well, let them watch until their eyeballs popped; let them listen until their eardrums buckled. Who cared? Who gave a damn?

There were four heavy wooden chairs and an old wooden table with a badly scarred top that looked like it'd been dragged out of some alley—the only furniture in the room. A bare light bulb hung over the table. Tate sat in one of the chairs. A fat detective with sleepy eyes and his shirtsleeves rolled meticulously up to the elbow sat across the table, opposite him. Another detective, this one skinny, in a wrinkled sweater and baggy pants, stood nearby, turning a pack of cigarettes over and over in one hand. *Mutt and Jeff*, Tate thought. *Laurel and Hardy—*

The fat detective said, "Mr. Tate, we'd like you to answer some questions."

Tate said nothing. Absently, he reached up and touched his cheek. There was a puffy gauze and tape dressing on it. One on his chin as well. *Vaguely, he remembered the police officers. The nurses. The doctor. Tate had been lying down under a bright light on a table covered with paper that rustled beneath him; then he'd sat up. The doctor had said: "You'll be all right, Mr. Tate. There's nothing broken. Just bruises and some scratches. And you had a bit of a fainting spell. You'll be fine ..."*

"What about Margie?"

"Margie?"

"My wife. Will she pull through, doctor? Is she going to live?"

The doctor had given him a blank look. "I'm sorry, but I don't understand—"

Tate did. He buried his face in his hands.

"Mr. Tate—"

"Eh—?"

"Please, Mr. Tate, pay attention. We need your cooperation. Answer the questions—"

"Ask them."

The seated detective tapped the table gently. "You're here as a tourist—"

"I'm a visitor. There's a difference, you know."

"How long did you intend to be in the country?"

Tate shrugged. "Two weeks. Ten days. I don't remember."

The questioner cleared his throat. "Your wife—" he began.

Tate cut him off: "Don't mention my wife. I forbid it!"

The detective who stood came closer to the table. "All right," he said in a subdued tone, "we won't talk about your wife. Just tell us what happened this morning—"

Tate leaned back in the chair. "Why?"

The standing detective glanced at his partner and then back again at Tate. "So we can get things straight, that's why."

"Straight?" Tate smiled. "Don't you know that the world is crooked? Haven't you learned that by now?"

"Never mind the philosophy," said the seated detective. "Tell us why you attacked the Arab."

Tate was silent.

"I repeat: why did you attack the Arab with a knife?"

"I wanted to kill him," said Tate placidly. "To rid the earth of his presence. To pack him off to Allah …"

"Then you did intend to kill him?"

"Yes."

"Did you know him?"

"Yes."

"How … did you know him?"

"God introduced me."

The standing detective pulled a chair out and sat down. He took a cigarette from the package. "Why did you want to kill him?"

Tate shook his head. "I'm surprised at you! Really! He's my enemy, of course. He's your enemy, too. Is that so difficult a concept to grasp? Doesn't your Talmud tell you: 'The person who comes to kill you—kill him first!'? Good advice, I'd say. Have you forgotten it? Killing isn't murder, after all. You should know that. The commandment reads: 'Thou shalt not *murder*,' not 'Thou shalt not *kill*.' The Christians have got it all wrong. It was mistranslated. I read about it once. But you fellows ought to know. You're Jewish, aren't you?"

The thin detective put the cigarette in his mouth.

Tate watched him light it. "You shouldn't smoke," he said. "You'll live longer if you quit. Be able to interrogate more people. Ask more questions. Catch more criminals—"

The smoker lifted a chip of tobacco from his tongue. "Please, Mr. Tate. Cooperate with us. This isn't a fencing match or a Ping-Pong game. Stick to what you're asked. Can you do that, Mr. Tate?"

Tate folded his arms across his chest. "Of course I can!" He laughed. "When all is said and done, didn't I come down from the stratosphere? From outer space to earth? All by my lonesome, without the help of a spaceship?" He pointed a finger at his questioners. It felt good to be questioning them. "Christ multiplied the loaves and the fish. He turned water into wine. But I—Alan Tate—converted flesh into steel! Top that one, if you can!"

The thin detective stubbed his cigarette out in a dull, metal ashtray. "Mr. Tate—"

"You've stopped smoking," Tate exclaimed cheerfully. "That takes will power! Good for you!"

* * *

In the little chamber behind the one-way mirror, Deputy Inspector Yechezkiel Bar-Am stroked his chin. "What an odd one," he said. "Do you think he's a looney?"

Chief Inspector Amnon Kochavi shrugged. He rose slowly from his seat. "These days," he said, "what's looney?"

* * *

They kept him in a lockup overnight. So this was jail, eh? Well, it wasn't that bad, wasn't that bad at all. He could take it. He had come from the outer hem of the galaxy all the way to Earth. Without a space suit. Without anybody's help. He could take it. He could do anything. If he wanted. If he wanted to want.

He was by himself. All by his lonesome. Well, that was all right, too. OK with him. He could manage it. If the Prisoner of Zenda, the Man in the Iron Mask, and the Birdman of Alcatraz could hack it, so could he. Wasn't he Alan Tate, Conqueror of Space and Master of the Great Hunting Knife Illusion? What they had to dish out, he could take. And then some. Sock it right back to them! Knock their eyeballs out! Set their teeth on edge! He chuckled. The authorities had quizzed him. Grilled him like a hamburger. Gotten nowhere with him. Determined that he was uncooperative. That he was evasive. Stubborn. Fork-tongued, if he were permitted the expression. Hadn't Deputy Inspector Yechezkiel ("Chezzie," the others called him, but Tate would never do it—he respected full names; he hated nicknames) Bar-Am said so himself? Come right out with it? No nonsense. Straight from the shoulder. "Mr. Tate, I'm afraid that you're not being cooperative with us. We shall have to hold you. Would you like to contact an attorney? We'll arrange it for you." Tate shook his head. "Don't need a lawyer," he told the Deputy Inspector. "God is my lawyer. He works pro bono, you know." Bar-Am had frowned. "You're sparring with us, Tate," he said. "Playing cat and mouse. Hide-and-seek. We don't like it, Tate. Not a bit." Came straight out and said it. Just like that. No skirting the issue. No pussyfooting around. No bullshit. Well, that wasn't bad, either. In fact, Tate rather liked it. Admired it. Could even see their point of view. The police wanted hard facts, biteable coins, bottom lines. And he had served them up cornmeal mush, Jell-O with whipped cream. But there was always tomorrow; they were welcome to try again …

He yawned. Covered his mouth when he did, from force of habit. It was ingrained. Margie always made him cover his mouth when he yawned. He closed his eyes. Felt his consciousness draining away. What a relief! "Good night, Margie," he murmured, scarcely able to form the words. And then, sitting upright on the wooden bench suspended by chains from the wall, he fell sound asleep. *How about that*?

Jerusalem, December 29, 1992
Central Police Station
6:40 am

"How about that?" he thought in the morning when they brought in his breakfast. The tray it came on was tin, but the eating utensils were plastic. So he couldn't kill himself, no doubt. Or anyone else. "Watch out for that guy, Tate," someone must have said. "He's got a passion for knives." It wasn't true; there was only a utilitarian attachment.

He sat on the bench with the tray on his lap. There were scrambled eggs, cucumber, tomato, and pepper salad, pita, margarine, and java. As he ate, he stared at the graffiti on the walls. Then they came for him. Two tight-lipped guards. "Hey," he protested. "I didn't get to finish my coffee—"

They brought him to the green room again, apparently to begin where they'd left off. This time, the lineup was different. The fat detective was there, seated at the table, looking glum. Beside him was none other than Deputy Inspector Yechezkiel Bar-Am.

"Where is he?" said Tate as he sat down in his place.

"Where is who?" said the fat detective.

"The guy who smoked," said Tate. He put up a hand. "Never mind," he said. "I know where he is. The smoking killed him."

Deputy Inspector Bar-Am leaned forward. He had thin, prematurely gray hair and a football-shaped, lumpy-featured face that looked like it had been arc-welded together. He had a low forehead, and his eyes had the hard, unrelenting stare of a fanatic. "Tate," he said, "I'm going to be very frank with you. My patience has run out. I'm mad. Quit the damn stalling, Tate. Who put you up to attacking that Arab?"

"I already told you. God—"

"Why that particular Arab?"

"He was there, that's why."

"He was where?"

"On the spot—"

"On what spot?"

"I already told you. I won't discuss it. You hear? You get it? I'm mad, too. My patience is running out."

"All right," said Bar-Am. "I hear you." His voice softened. "What did you intend to do after … you killed the Arab?"

Tate relaxed. "That's an easy one," he said: "Kill more Arabs."

"Kill more? How many more?"

"As many as possible. Clear the street of them."

"And then?"

Tate was silent.

"And then, Tate. Answer me, please."

Tate sighed. He put his hands up on the table and folded them. Wasn't the teacher talking to him?

Bar-Am took hold of his chin. Tightly, as if it might fly off. He stared at Tate as though he were looking at a specimen through a microscope, uncertain as to what it might do ... .

Jerusalem, December 30, 1992
Psychiatric Ward
Mt. Zion Hospital
9:11 am

A white room. This time, they'd stuck him in a room painted white. Why had they done it? He was used to green, so why had they put him in white?

"… *as white as driven snow* …"

Ah, that was it …

"Though thy sins be scarlet,
They shall be white as driven snow—"

Yes, that was certainly it; they were telling him something. Because everywhere he turned was white. He hummed a few bars of "White Christmas." When he was very small, his family had sung it around the tree. He hated the song (so why did he hum it now; why did it stick in his mind like stale chewing gum?), but his sister Jennifer had loved it; and what Jennifer loved, Daddy did. Axiomatic. Then he hummed, "White, white, white is the color of my true love's hair." He didn't remember all the words, but that was OK. And there was something wrong with the way he'd construed the title, but who cared? As long as his intent was honest …

Then he sang—sang, not hummed—"The White Cliffs of Dover." Right out loud. This one he had down pat:

"There'll be love and laughter,
And peace ever after …"

Hah! He remembered all the words, every last one of them. He was proud of himself. Justly so. He threw back his head and belted the song out:

"… *and Sarah will go to sleep*
in her own little room again …"

Wait a minute. Hold on. That wasn't right. It was "Jimmy." Sarah belonged to his life: and she would never sleep in her own, little room again. It was "Jimmy" he'd wanted to sing:

" … and Jimmy will go to sleep
in his own little room again …"

He had just finished singing when the man in the white suit walked in. Tate had to laugh. "Are you Alec Guinness?" he asked.

"Alec Guinness? What are you talking about?"

"You know, "The Man in the White Suit". He was the star. It was a terrific film. I saw it with Margie. A long time ago …"

"I never saw the film," the newcomer said. He smiled. "And I'm certainly not Sir Alec Guinness!"

"Then who are you?"

"My name is Schechter. Dr. Bernard Schechter."

Tate stared at the man. He was about forty-five, slim and pleasant-looking, with curly brown hair and a dimple in his chin. He wore glasses: they were framed in tortoise-shell and could have been a perfect match for Margie's comb and pocket mirror. But the comb and mirror were gone. Tossed into the wastebasket. Dumped into the collective trash of the hotel. Carted away. Gone forever.

"I'm Dr. Bernard Schechter," the newcomer repeated.

Tate nodded. "Well, then, I'll call you Bernard. Never Bernie. You can rely on me—"

"And you're Alan Tate …"

"Yes. Call me Alan. Not Al. I hate Al. Always have."

The doctor extended a hand.

Tate stared at it. "The hand of Jacob? Or the hand of Esau? Or the "'hand that struck the tyrant dead … and became the tyrant in its stead?'"

"It's my own hand. Try it."

Tate did. "At least you speak English decently," he said. "Not like that other doctor. The one with the bushy eyebrows and the goatee—"

"Dr. Ben-Ami—"

"Ben-Ami, salami—who gives a damn? He butchers the English language into pieces; that's what counts …"

"Well, Alan, you certainly won't have any problem with me. I'm from Chicago—born and bred there. I spent ten years at a major psychiatric hospital there. I was head of my section."

Tate was silent. He looked down at himself. "Tell me," he said, raising his eyes. "Why am I all trussed up this way?"

"You mean the straightjacket?"

"Whatever it's called—"

"You don't remember being violent? Throwing furniture around? Punching Inspector Bar-Am? Taking a swing at the admitting doctor here? Wrestling with the orderlies?" Schechter waved a hand. "And the list goes on, I'm afraid—"

"Did I do all those things?"

"You don't recall?"

Tate shook his head.

"Well, you really did them, Alan. I promise you."

"Shame on me!"

Schechter was silent for a moment. Then he said: "Alan, do you know why you were arrested in the first place?"

Tate looked into the doctor's eyes. Scrutinized them. They were light gray and flecked with green. Tate thought there was softness in them all right, even kindness. But he had to be wary. Wasn't Schechter's pleasantness only a screen for something cold and calculating that lay behind it? Something made of high-grade surgical steel—like the hunting knife. Something machinelike that coaxed people into it and then snapped shut unexpectedly and trapped them. Tate considered carefully; it was necessary. So many tricks had been played on him lately—dirty tricks—that he had to watch out. Had to be on his guard. Couldn't let himself be caught. He swallowed the saliva in his mouth. "Why the police arrested me? Is that what you're asking?"

"Yes, Alan. Do you remember why?"

"Sure I do—" Tate clucked his tongue. "And I can tell you. But you won't understand."

"Why won't I understand?"

"Because you're not Jewish, that's why."

"I'm afraid you've got things a little mixed up, Alan," Schechter gestured. "I'm Jewish; you're not."

Tate was visibly annoyed. "I most certainly do not have things mixed up," he said firmly. "I know very well that I'm not Jewish. The point I'm making is that *you're* not! Maybe you once were, but you're not anymore. You've turned Christian, like Bar-Am and Kochavi and the rest of them. They believe in turning the other cheek. They didn't understand what I was doing, so they arrested me. You people don't understand me, so you stick me in your mental hospital. In this damn white room! And I hate white! It reminds me of the white whale. Have you read *Moby Dick*? Poor Melville. Writes a book like that and people didn't like it when it came out. It alienated his readers. His ratings went down—"

Dr. Schechter adjusted his glasses. "Alan, tell me why you tried to stab that Arab on Salah-ed-din Street."

Tate's face tightened. His mouth clamped shut. But suddenly, without his wanting or expecting it, it popped open. "All right, Bernard," he said hoarsely, "you're not a nice guy—however much you seem to be a nice guy—and you're not Jewish any longer, though you like to pretend you are, but I'll tell you anyway. For old time's sake. It'll do me good. Get it off my chest. Give my soul an enema—" He threw back his head and laughed. But the laugh turned to a cry and the cry to a wail.

Schechter moved toward him.

"Don't come near me!" Tate screamed. "Give me my knife! Where's my hunting knife? I bought it in the camping goods store up on Hillel Street! It's mine! I want it back! I've got to finish my work! Give it to me—"

Dr. Schechter gave him a shot.

* * *

The nurse smiled. Pretty nurse. Pretty smile. "Feeling better, Mr. Tate?"

He sat up. "Better than what?"

"The doctor will be here in just a few minutes ..."

The nurse went out. And sure enough, the man in the white coat walked in. Brisk. Chipper. Bright-eyed and bushy-tailed. A good doctor. Full of good news. "Good morning, Alan," he said airily, "and how are we today?" There was a chair in the room. He sat down.

Tate looked at himself. "Hey," he said. "I just noticed. I'm loose. Free. Unfettered. No straightjacket. What happened?"

"Nothing much," said Schechter. "I've decided to trust you, Alan. That's all."

"That simple, eh?"

"That simple." Schechter smiled. Nice smile, really. Clean-cut. Friendly. Trusting. "Feel like talking today?"

"Could be—"

Schechter crossed one leg over the other. Nice pants. Creased to the millimeter. Shiny shoes. Two-tone oxfords. Classy socks, too. "Well," the doctor said amiably, "I suppose I can regard that as a 'yes.' A guarded 'yes,' one might say, but a 'yes' nevertheless." He stroked his cheek. "All right, then. How's about starting up where you left off the other day? Remember? You were telling me about the Arab ..."

"You're married?" said Tate.

"Excuse me—"

"Just now, when you reached up to scratch your cheek, I saw your wedding ring ..."

Schechter nodded. "Yes, Alan. As a matter of fact, I'm married. Why do you mention it?"

Tate stared at him for a time and then glanced away. He looked to the window, through whose gray wire mesh sunlight trickled onto the bright tile floor. Then he faced back. "No reason," he said. "No reason at all." He cleared his throat. "So that Arab bugs you, eh, Bernard? You'd like to know all about him, would you? What is there to say, Bernard? The Arabs are like the Nazis, only they don't have German technology—"

"Alan—"

Tate shook his head. "But I don't really want to discuss the fiasco on Salah-ed-din Street. It was a waste. The police interfered. And now you people have butted in. Poked your damn noses into my business—"

"Alan, you're throwing up a smokescreen. Don't—"

"Xanadu ... and Xanadon't!" Tate sputtered. He laughed. "Listen, my dear doctor," he said. "This is the way it is: God sits at the piano, running His fingers over the keyboard of our days and nights. Tickling the ivories of time-and-tide. And when He gets tired, He stops. Slams the piano lid down. Bang! Throws the sheet music on the floor. Whop! Stomps on it with His seven-league boots. *Clump-clump-clump*! And we humans are done for, ended, finished. Fin comes onto the screen—" Tate paused to catch his breath. "But you look perplexed, Bernard. Perhaps you'd like me to explain—"

And without waiting for an answer, Tate went on: "You see, Bernard, it was this way: God and I were playing cards. 'Show me Your hand,' I say to Him—"

"'Fat chance of that,' says He."

"'No, no' say I: 'I mean it. Honest injun. Show me Your hand.'"

"'It ain't in the cards,' says He. And He bursts out laughing. 'That there's a joke,' says He: 'You're supposed to laugh, too—'"

"Say I: 'I don't see anything funny. This is serious stuff. Show me what's in Your hand. Be a Sport.'"

"So then God thinks for a moment—or a millennium or eon or whatever time He goes by. And then, believe it or not, He pulls the cards away from His chest and slaps them down on the table. 'There,' He says: 'You asked for it, so don't complain.'"

"'But You've got all the aces!' I say."

"And God shrugs. 'That's the game,' He says: 'Take it or leave it!'"

Tate leaned back on his pillow.

"Are you finished?" asked Schechter evenly.

"Yes. Quite finished."

"May I ask you a question?"

"Why not? After all, you're the doctor …"

Schechter uncrossed his legs and leaned forward. "Did attacking the Arab have anything to do … with your wife?"

Tate stiffened. "My wife is dead," he said.

"I know that," said Schechter softly. "I know all about that and I'm terribly grieved—"

Tate interrupted: "But we're still married," he said. "As married as you and your wife …" He drew the sheet to his chest. "But Margie's my business. Not yours. Keep your questions off her. Understand?"

"Alan—"

"Don't 'Alan' me, Bernard!"

"You must talk about your wife."

"Not a word. Not a single, blessed word!"

"Alan—"

Tate snapped the sheet from his body. "Get out of here, Bernard," he growled: "Or I'll throw you out!"

And Schechter knew he would.

* * *

In the staff lounge, Schechter sipped coffee from a paper cup that let the heat through.

"How's he doing?"

Schechter turned. Ben-Ami was there—bushy eyebrows, goatee, and all. Schechter smiled to himself. Ben-Ami, salami, he thought.

"Well, how's he doing?"

Schechter knew perfectly well whom the other man was referring to. Nevertheless, he asked, "How is who doing?"

"The American. The one who tried to knife the Arab. What's his name—Cape?"

"Tate."

"Ah, yes. Of course. Mr. Tate. The Savior of the Third Jewish Commonwealth." He picked a crumb from his upper lip. "The two hundredth …"

"Two hundredth? What the devil are you talking about?"

"It's almost the end of the year. Mr. Tate is the two hundredth person to be afflicted with the 'Jerusalem Syndrome.' I checked the records when I came in this morning."

Schechter stared at him. "Who told you he's afflicted with anything but grief?" he wanted to ask.

But he said nothing.

*   *   *

The door swung open, but Tate had his back toward it. Schechter had been in already that morning, so it wasn't Schechter. Like the postman, he never came twice—or had Tate mixed it all up? What matter—it was probably another pretty nurse. Tate disliked beautiful nurses; they reminded him of the fading beauty of the world.

He rolled over and looked. It wasn't a nurse at all; it was an old man. How strange! Tate didn't know any old man; perhaps the newcomer had come in by mistake. Tate sat up. "You're in the wrong room," he called out. "You don't want me. I'm Alan Tate. The Arab-killer. Savior of the Jews—"

But the old man came stubbornly forward. Slowly, because he was a very old man. He was nearly bent double, and he walked with a cane. Tate heard it: tap-tap-tap on the freshly scrubbed tile floor. Tate felt a sharp pang at his heart, but he had no idea why. "Hey," he called out. "What are you doing in here? Who are you?"

"Don't you recognize me?"

Tate shook his head. "No. Should I?"

With obvious difficulty, the old man pulled the chair up to Tate's cot and seated himself. When he was stable, he leaned forward and said: "Now, look at me, Tate. Up close."

"Dr. Hadashi!"

"Yes, yes. Shmuel Hadashi. Come to see you, my dear friend—"

Tate stared at the newcomer. "But—but you're ancient," he blurted out. "You remind me of the parchment that Margie and I saw in the Shrine of the Book! What happened to you, Hadashi?"

The other man said nothing. He remained silent for several moments. Then he pulled himself together. Resting his rope-veined hands on the head of his cane, he said softly, "Why didn't you call me, Alan? Why didn't you let me know?"

Tate looked away. Beyond the metal grating over the window, sunlight danced merrily. "I—I don't remember," he said thickly. "I don't know why I forgot to telephone you. I forget … so many things these days. You'll have to forgive me. Or don't forgive me, if you wish. Who cares?"

"Alan," persisted Hadashi's soft voice. "Why didn't you contact me?"

With his eyes still averted, Tate said, "I did call you. Several times. You didn't answer."

"I was away for a couple of days. Visiting with a friend, up north. In Nof Ginossar, as a matter of fact. You could've reached me after I returned."

Tate faced back to his guest. "Ah, Nof Ginossar ..." He smiled. "I remembered what you'd said, and made reservations at the hotel there. For Margie and me—"

"I called the hotel, Alan. The manager—"

Tate cut him off. "You see, you wasted your time, Hadashi. You never should have bothered to help us look for that contact lens in the museum. Margie doesn't need it now. She sees everything. Without any lenses. Perfectly. How about that?"

"The manager on duty told me everything. About dear Mrs. Tate—" Hadashi broke off. His hands shook. He tried to resume speaking, but couldn't do it. He placed a hand over his eyes. When he felt steady, he uncovered his eyes. Tate was on his back, with the blanket drawn over his head. "Alan?" said Hadashi.

There was no answer.

Hadashi sighed. Painfully, he rose. Tap-tap-tap—his cane struck the floor. At the door, he glanced once again at the inert figure under the blanket. "That's all right," he murmured. "I'll be back."

But he might as well have been speaking to the dead.

* * *

Hadashi twisted on the chair. He pulled a handkerchief from his pocket and carefully wiped his lips. "I told you that I'd be back," he said, returning the handkerchief to its place.

"So you're back. So what do you want me to do about it?"

"Just talk to me, Alan. That's all."

"What do you want me to say?"

Hadashi's voice dropped. "Tell me why you tried to knife that Arab."

Tate's eyes hardened. He drew a deep breath. "So that's it," he said fiercely. "You're a policeman. A detective. You've gone over to the camp of the gentiles too, damn you!"

"Alan, you know better. You know very well who I am."

"Then why do you ask me that question?"

"Because I want to understand you."

"Understand me? For what purpose?"

"So I can help you."

Tate threw back his head and laughed. The laugh was like a bark—so loud and so harsh that, despite his best resolve, his guest started visibly. Well, what was Tate supposed to do? That was the penalty of coming to see him. Tate shook his head. "Help me?" he said. "What a preposterous idea! You can't help me. No one in this big, ugly world can help me. Or himself, for that matter."

"Give me a chance, Alan. All I want is a chance. Just tell me why you tried to kill the Arab."

"You really want to know, eh?"

"Yes."

"And you're really my friend?"

"Very much so."

Tate's eyes narrowed. "And you can't guess the reason?"

"I can guess lots of things, Alan. But I'd like you to tell me yourself ..."

Tate sat in silence. In his mind, a signpost pointed in opposite directions: to remain silent or to talk. Decisions were hard, but he had to decide. There was no one to advise him. He could speak to Margie—she always understood—but she couldn't answer. There was no two-way hookup. What could he do? He stared at his guest. Hadashi seemed half of what he'd been. There was a bleakness about him, as if he walked around in perpetual shadow. He seemed on his way—where to, Tate did not care to consider. But Hadashi was patient. Oh, yes. Patient and kind: he hadn't lost those attributes, despite his weariness. It was too bad that patience and kindness weren't enough. That wasn't Tate's fault. So many things were not his fault. *Then whose were they?*

Tate fiddled with the edge of the blanket; he reached around and propped up the pillow behind his back. He wanted to appear alive. It wouldn't do for him to be taken for a corpse. Why, he didn't exactly know, but what the hell, he couldn't know everything! "All right," he said at length, "I'm ready to spill the beans. For you, Hadashi, because you're my friend."

"Thank you, Alan."

"Well, the Arab on Salah-ed-din Street was the first one on my list. After I cut his throat—" Tate paused to watch Hadashi's reaction. But there was nothing—not the flicker of an eyelash. He sat, gnarled hands resting on the head of his cane, with a composed, expressionless face. "Well," Tate went on, "after that, I intended to stab others. You see, I started at the spot where Margie was hit by the rock. I knew exactly where it was—as if I could ever forget! And then I planned to go up the street, stabbing them as I went. Mowing them down. Blasting them to bits. No half measures. All the way to the Great Mosque. Margie despised that mosque, you know. Thought it was tacky. Can you blame her?"

Still, Hadashi sat without expression, without a word. He looked like a pile of old clothing on the chair. Like flotsam the waves had washed up.

"Are you asleep?" Tate asked.

"No, Alan."

Hadashi's voice was weak. Little more than audible breath. A feather. A wisp. Tate shook his head. What a pity. What a damn shame. Another sputter or two and his guest would go out. For good. Like the candles on the Chanukah lamp.

But Hadashi's voice came again—and it wasn't weak. "What about Margie, Alan? Tell me about your wife."

In a flash, the gray hospital blanket went up and over Tate's head. He looked like a mummy. But at least he wasn't flat on his back.

Tel Aviv, January 8, 1993
Vitkin Street
1:16 am

The ticking of the grandfather clock seemed to fill the entire apartment. Usually, Hadashi didn't notice it—it was like a second pulse—but tonight he could not escape it. "*Tate—Tate—Tate—*" it seemed to say. Or to warn. The blinds were down and the heavy drapes drawn shut, so that the bedroom was in total darkness: Hadashi might have been encased in a bathysphere, two or three kilometers below the surface of the ocean. Except for the diabolical ticking of the clock.

He had been trying to fall asleep for a couple of hours, but—like some cunning quarry—sleep had eluded him. He turned from side to side, lay on his back and then on his stomach. Nothing availed. At length, he sat up and swung his legs out of bed. By feel, he fitted his feet into his house slippers. Then he moved blindly over the familiar carpet route to the closet. He took out his robe and donned it. When he opened the bedroom door, the ticking seemed to explode down the hallway. He crossed the living room. The clock played its silvery introduction to the hour and chimed. *Four*, it announced: "*Tate—Tate—Tate—Tate.*"

Through the kitchen window, yellow-white light came in from a street lamp. It was enough for him to see by; he didn't have to press a switch. He filled the kettle with water, and placed it on a burner to boil. He stood close to the range, round-backed and scarecrowlike in his faded robe and unraveling slippers. Absently, a hand reached up and grazed the stubble on his cheek. He sighed. Thus far, he had visited Tate twice in the hospital. He had spoken with the staff. With Ben-Ami, who was useless—a blusterer and a blunderer. With Marion Bookbinder, who had seen Tate a number of times and come away concluding that he had been mentally unstable all his life and "would never, in all probability, climb out of the pit he'd been digging for decades." And with Schechter, who was both well trained and a *mensch* to boot. But Schechter was overloaded—precisely because he was so good—and wouldn't be able to give Tate the required time and attention. That left—

The kettle boiled. Steam shot up from its spout. Like the petals of some ghostly blossom. Hadashi watched for a few seconds: nature was filled with drama, if not art. He shut off the stove and filled his cup. Seated at the small, oilcloth-covered table, he brooded. He knew that Tate was on a tightrope and could go either way. Back into the world that men, for lack of—or because they dreaded—another word, called "sane" or else, into the abyss. Hadashi lifted his cup and sipped the strong, hot tea into which he had dropped three sugar cubes. He also knew that the list of doctors he'd mentally crossed off left—himself. It was up to him. That is, it was up to Tate, but it was up to Hadashi to get that point across.

When he finished drinking the tea, he rose and put the cup in the sink. The tap leaked and he reminded himself that he had to have it fixed. Slippers scuffing over the floor, he left the kitchen. Again, he had the feeling of being underwater; the living room was like the rotting hull of a ship sunk ages ago. He shuffled past the grandfather clock; its ticking pursued him down the hallway. He visited the bathroom and emerged fumbling with his robe. At the bedroom doorway, he halted. There was faint illumination and he was able to make out the furniture: the bed in which he'd slept with his wife and in which his only son had been conceived, the dresser to the right on whose top were ranged a dozen or more framed photographs from years fallen into the dust, the oversized armchair in the corner. He entered, but did not close the door behind him. He threw the robe onto the chair, sat down on the bed, and kicked off his slippers. He got under the quilt and put his head down on the pillow. The clock ticked. "*Tate,*" it said over and over again.

"All right," he said. "I know. But I'm tired. *So very tired …*"

Jerusalem, January 9, 1993
Psychiatric Ward
Mt. Zion Hospital
10:30 am

Down at the end of the brightly lit corridor was the small sun parlor. There wasn't any sun today, but they didn't change the name. "Your visitor's waiting for you there," the nurse said to Tate as she steered him.

"Visitor? I don't get visitors. Hadashi comes to see me, but he's my friend—not a visitor. Nobody else ever comes. Even the detectives and the cops have quit. How could I have a visitor?"

The nurse smiled. "I'm sure you'll know this man when you see him."

Tate did. "Sperris! Reverend Sperris! What in the name of heaven are you doing here?"

Tate hadn't seen Sperris since he and Margie had left him and their church group to pursue their own journey through Israel the morning after they landed at Ben Gurion Airport. The Reverend was round as a butterball and dressed to the nines, with matching corduroy jacket and trousers and a sporty hat with a feather in it that he'd neglected to take off. He jumped up from his chair. "Alan! My dear, dear Alan!"

"Don't touch me," said Tate.

The two of them sat facing each other in front of the center window, bathed in the light of a gray Jerusalem. The nurse sat across the room from them, swinging one leg over the other and leafing through a Hebrew magazine.

"Since there were no next of kin who could be contacted …" Sperris was saying.

Tate hadn't really been listening, but at these words his ears perked up. "What was that?"

"I was remarking, my dear Alan, that, since there were no next of kin I could reach, I was compelled to make all the necessary arrangements. The people at the Embassy down on Hayarkon Street were so very helpful. Especially one of the vice-consuls, who was remarkably kind. His name was … let me see—"

"What arrangements?" said Tate.

Sperris, who looked fatter, sleeker, and more impressed with himself than ever, stared at him. So, looking up from the magazine, did the nurse.

"*What* arrangements?" Tate demanded.

Sperris seemed surprised. "Why, for shipping the body back to the States, of course. And for burial—"

"*Whose* body?" Tate said ominously, rising from the chair.

Sperris was nonplussed. "Why, why … Margie's, of course." His plump, polished face turned white. He glanced over at the nurse, who had also risen. "I thought—" he sputtered. "That is, they told me he—"

He tried to get up, but Tate's hands were at his neck, ramming him back onto the chair with such force that it tipped. "Help—" Sperris choked. "Please … someone … *help!*"

"Give me back my Margie!" Tate was screaming. "You had no right to take her! She's my wife! She's mine! Give her back!"

"Orderly!" shouted the nurse, rushing forward.

*   *   *

Now, there were two chairs in the white room, the Moby Dick room, the "White Cliffs of Dover" room. Tate sat on one. Opposite him, Hadashi sat on the other.

Tate grinned. "The Rover Boys," he said.

"Excuse me?"

"Abbott and Costello …"

Hadashi shook his head.

"Groucho and Harpo …"

"I don't follow, Alan."

"Amos and Andy," said Tate. He exploded into laughter.

Hadashi's expression was severe. "Alan, what is this all about?"

Tate waved a hand. "Nothing," he said. "Nothing important …" He bowed his head. "Forgive me, Father," he intoned, "for I know not what You do …"

Hadashi's thin, bloodless lips clamped together. His cheeks twitched. Evenly, as if shifting gears in a car, he moved the head of the cane to and fro and from side to side. Then he stabilized it. "See here, Alan," he said in a voice that flowed like slow, sweet sap. "See here, my dear friend. "I gave a lot of thought to what you said the first time I came. About my being 'ancient'." The expression in his eyes was earnest, importunate. "You were right. Absolutely. I am … ancient, just as you observed." His voice blurred and he cleared his throat. "The news … the terrible, terrible news—what happened to your dear, lovely wife—" He stopped, raised a hand to his eyes and dropped it. "Alan, I have neither the strength nor the patience nor, perhaps, the time to dance the minuet or quadrille or tango with you. I'm weary, my friend, worn out. This last, ghastly storm of life has blown a hole in me that will not repair. That's why I'll speak directly to you. No strategy. No planned approach. Just directness. A synapse across the void, so to speak." He leaned forward. "Alan, madness has crept into you, like a worm. It gnaws at you now. In the end, it will devour you altogether. That is, if you permit it to do so. You have the power, Alan, the power to pull that worm out, to kill it. I know you have the power; and, more important, you know that you've the power. It's that clear-cut. It's that simple. What you need is the will. Did you hear me?"

Tate had indeed heard. He had even understood. His mind, as though it were on a rusty hinge, had creaked. But the door failed to open.

"Alan—"

"Tweedledum and Tweedledee," said Tate. And he roared with laughter.

Jerusalem, January 23, 1993
Psychiatric Ward
Mt. Zion Hospital
2:05 pm

The two of them were sitting in the sun parlor. The day was bright. Light streamed in through the windows; it looked like someone had carved chunks out of the sun and scattered them over the floor. Hadashi's spotted fingers twisted the head of the cane. "You know, Alan, I've been coming here now for almost three weeks."

Tate nodded. "Good. Come here as long as you want. As often as you want. Sleep over, if you wish. The cots are comfortable. The food's not bad. The nurses are pretty. The doctors … well, the doctors leave much to be desired, but what the devil—you can't have everything!"

"Alan—"

"Yes …"

"Alan, you know all that's not the point."

Tate felt his mind spin like a roulette wheel; the little white ball just wouldn't stop. "The point is the counter," he said. "One of the Huxley family wrote that. Also, 'the medium is the message.' Marshall somebody said it. General George Marshall. Or maybe Field Marshall Montgomery. An army man, for sure. Or maybe not? Maybe it was Marshall Field—" He shrugged. "Somebody. It couldn't have been said by nobody—"

Hadashi leaned forward. "Stop it," he said. "I won't have it anymore. I *can't* have it anymore. I've come to see you these weeks in good faith. But I no longer have the strength or the faith. If you don't stop this, Alan, I'm not coming back."

"What?"

"You heard me. If you don't cut this nonsense out, you're on your own. Stay here in the hospital. Rot here. Disappear into thin air here. I don't give a damn what you do. It's not my affair."

Tate was silent. His hands gripped the arms of his chair. He turned his head. Through the windows, Jerusalem's rooftops gleamed with restless fire. To the east, the mountains repeated themselves, like petrified waves. He blinked. There were tears in his mind, but not in his eyes. Had the spinning roulette wheel slowed? It was hard for him to tell. But for the first time, he wished it would.

"Alan, look at me—"

Tate looked at him.

"Remember: this isn't an idle warning. I won't come back—"

Tate swallowed the lump in his throat.

"Margie. Your beloved wife. Your dear partner. She's dead. Dead, Alan, and on her way to burial. Understand?"

There was silence. From down the corridor, voices broke into it for a time; they faded and the silence returned. The two men sat opposite each other like two blocks of granite. Hadashi bit his lip. He had just made the decision to get up and go when Tate said: "I understand."

"She will never return, Alan."

"No."

"You will never see her again, except in your memory and in your dreams."

"No."

"And you cannot avenge her death by killing Arabs at random."

"No."

"Then—" Hadashi waved a hand. "Then all of this—this impropriety is finished. Ended. Put to rest."

"Yes," said Tate.

He meant it. *The roulette wheel had stopped turning. The little white ball had popped into place.*

* * *

"Have something," said Schechter.

Hadashi shook his head. "No, thanks. I'm not really hungry."

The two men were in the hospital cafeteria, moving toward the cashier. Schechter had filled his tray with plates. His smile was almost apologetic. "I'm off my bloody diet at long last," he said. "Really," he added. "Take something, Shmuel. The onion soup is very good here."

"I'll have a cup of coffee," said Hadashi.

They sat in the staff room, to the rear of the large hall. "So," said Schechter, rolling spaghetti onto a spoon, "you waved a wand and—"

"No wand," interrupted Hadashi, "no magic. I told him that if he continued to act out I wasn't coming back—and I wasn't—and he got the point. No more diversions. No more evasions. No more circus tricks. I'd had enough. And I hoped he'd also had enough. That's all."

"Still and all, someone had to help him get the point."

Hadashi shrugged. "It really doesn't matter who or how. It's over. He's back. That's what counts."

Schechter nodded and broke a slice of rye bread in two. "And he's going to live with you?"

"Yes. For a while, at least. We're friends, you know." Hadashi put his cup down. "We are friends," he said. "Coming to live with me makes his release from the hospital easier. It makes sense. He doesn't want to return to the States. He has no place to go here—he's alone, really."

"I wasn't questioning it. I was just—"

"Questioning it," laughed Hadashi.

*   *   *

Dr. Ben-Ami glanced idly through the open door into the room. He had already gone past, but he backtracked to take a second look. A young man with snow-white hair was sitting on the bed, staring into empty air. Ben-Ami shook his head. "How odd," he mused, "how very odd."

Later in the day, he bumped into Schechter in the corridor. "Can it really be that Cape's out of here?"

"That who's out of here?"

"Sorry. I mean Tate, of course. The cowboy from the US of A. The Two Hundredth Messiah."

"Mr. Tate has been released from the hospital, yes," said Schechter coldly. "He left yesterday."

Ben-Ami pinched a bushy eyebrow. "I never would've let him go, you know—"

"The decision wasn't yours."

Ben-Ami cleared his throat. "And now he's on his way back to the Golden Land, eh? Well, he won't be Messiah there—that's for sure. They're already over their quota."

"As a matter of fact," said Schechter, turning to leave, "he's remaining in Israel."

"How odd," said Ben-Ami. "How very odd."

Tel Aviv, February 16, 1993
Promenade
8:45 am

The chairs were two of hundreds on the Tel Aviv boardwalk. They were white, plastic, durable, cheap.

But the view was rich: an unbroken expanse of Mediterranean. Emerald green and turquoise, with gashes of white that the dagger of the wind cut.

Not a major wind, though. A minor one, almost playful. Three days of rain had come to an end. The sun was out in an all but cloudless sky, gulls were coasting, mothers were out with their strollers, there were even several kites hopping about in the air, maneuvered by sweaterless stalwarts on the beach. It was mid-February, but the day was so fine that it might have been early spring.

The two men sat on chairs. They were side by side and so close that their shoulders almost touched. Even though the day was so mild, Hadashi wore an overcoat—hopelessly out of fashion, belted in the back—that came down almost to his ankles, a woolen muffler wound about his neck, and on his head a black beret pulled to one side. Tate had moved his belongings—not Margie's things, which he'd given to a local supply depot for new immigrants—from the hotel to Hadashi's apartment. Influenced by the pre-Christmas freeze in the Midwest, Margie had stuffed a leather jacket into a suitcase at the very last instant before their departure ("Who knows?" she'd commented. "Winter is winter, and Jerusalem's high up, isn't it?") Tate wore the jacket now. On his head, he wore a tan golfer's cap that he'd bought in a store on Allenby.

From time to time, the men spoke. It was part of an ongoing dialogue, in great part about the past. "We're a couple of mirrors," Hadashi said at one point, "reflecting backward …"

Tate smiled thinly. "We're not mirrors," he said. "We are … shadows …"

"So is life," said his companion.

They sat side by side, the glittering sea before them. *Turquoise*. The wind-whipped waves bared their teeth. *Emerald*. Swooping, the gulls dipped low and screamed. Far out, at the horizon, a ship moved almost indiscernibly, smoke from its stacks smudging the sky. A kite nose-dived, kicking up sand where it crashed. Hadashi tapped his cane on the pavement. "Memories," he observed. "They're like a string of worry beads. You take the string out and run your mind over the beads. Again and again. The same memory beads ..." He sighed. "Once in a while, you add a new one to the string."

Tate glanced at him. Hadashi looked like a ship whose sails had collapsed. Either the canvas was rent, or the wind had dropped. The result was just the same in both cases; the ship had lost its impetus.

When they'd sat long enough, they got up and traipsed along the boardwalk. Going south, the sea was on their right. On the left were the hotels: the Sheraton, and the Dan, whose waterfront facade was a gigantic painting by Agam comprised of geometric shapes in pastel colors; further down was the American Embassy, which—except for the satellite dish on the roof—looked like a medieval fortress.

They had their lunch in a little restaurant just off Dizengoff Boulevard. Olives, black and green. Cabbage salad. Mashed chickpeas with black beans, called *fool*. Hot pita with a spice called zatar. And sweet, black beer to wash it all down. As they ate, they talked about their lives. Childhood. Growing up. University: Tate in America's Midwest, Hadashi in Vienna and then in Jerusalem. Hadashi told the story of how he'd met his wife at a concert in Tel Aviv. Tate spoke of his encounter with Margie in the Student Union. By the time one of them glanced at a clock, more than two hours had flown by. "Two hours," said Tate. He snapped his fingers. "Twenty years. Just like that."

Hadashi scraped back his chair. "People lose track of time," he said, reaching out for his cane in the corner, "but time never loses track of people."

Back in the apartment, they discussed their respective weddings. Hadashi had married on a kibbutz lawn, under colored lights and among friends. Tate spoke of his furlough and the San Antonio justice of the peace, and of the almost immediate return to his army base. Hadashi trotted out half a dozen dusty photograph albums and brought all the framed pictures from the dresser in the bedroom into the living room. "The light's much better in here," he explained, turning the stiff pages eagerly. Tate had only the photos in his own and Margie's wallets. But he had the images in his mind and heart—and he gave of them freely.

Supper was light. They usually had it around six. The two men shopped together, most often in the large supermarket on Ben-Yehuda Street. They shared equally in the purchase of food and household goods. Tate offered to pay half the maintenance on the apartment. Hadashi refused summarily. "That's a foolish proposal," he told his guest almost with annoyance: "This is my place, and I'm the one who pays the maintenance. Shall I charge you for the bath water you use ... and for the air you breathe?"

They took turns preparing the meals they didn't eat out. It was Tate's turn that evening. He scrambled eggs, diced the vegetables for a salad, and sliced the fresh bread. Over the meal, they conversed about their children. Hadashi told stories about his paratrooper son. Tate related anecdotes about his daughter, Sarah. They nodded, gesticulated, smiled wistfully, and spoke out of turn as they reminisced. "The old string of memory beads, eh?" said Tate.

"Rub them well," observed Hadashi. "They're like Aladdin's lamp!"

After supper was finished and the dishwasher loaded, they listened to music on the stereo for a while—this evening, it was Mahler. Then they turned on the TV to watch a film. It was called *Mistress* and told the story of a writer approaching middle age in Los Angeles who gets a chance—so he believes—to have the screenplay he's struggled for seven years to sell … produced. Each of the film's three potential backers has a mistress who twists the script like taffy to suit her particular needs, confounding the poor, baffled, meat-grindered writer and punch-drunk producer. The film was a witty, gentle tragicomedy, and the two viewers laughed at the humor that came nimbly out of the pain. "Like the honey that came out of the lion's carcass that Samson found," suggested Hadashi.

They never discussed politics—"the art of the insane leading the demented," Hadashi termed it. And they never talked about religion. However, Tate did tell his friend that Margie had never wanted to "set foot in a church." Following which, Hadashi confided that his wife had never wished to go near a synagogue. "'God,' she always told me," said Hadashi, "'was wherever you found Him—if you were persistent in your search and prepared to stand the pain.'" He glanced toward the photographs on his desk. "'Pain is the raw material,' she once told me. 'The product is life.'"

* * *

Late one night, when neither one of them could sleep, they sat together at the kitchen table, and when Hadashi had finished an anecdote about his childhood, Tate leaned forward and after a prolonged silence told his friend a childhood story of his own, one which he had always in his mind called, "Jesus of the Woods." It had a lot to do with why he had come with Margie on this trip to Israel …

The child Alan was in the yard. Everything was white, and beyond the slats of the brown wood fence were enormous, unblemished drifts. In the distance, the evergreen woods seemed carved into the slate-gray sky. He was alone. Glad to be alone. In the house, they were listening to the radio and still fussing with the gifts. Through the living room window, he saw the colored lights of their Christmas tree flashing on and off, on and off. The tree, with its tinsel and painted glass, looked gaudy, trivial, irrelevant; it had embarrassed and discomfited him to be near it. Just as Jennifer's shrill "oohs" and "aahs" among the gift wrappings and ornamentation, his father's strident voice and bulldozer gestures, his mother's wispy apologies and downcast eyes had unsettled and pained him. Yes, it was better to be alone! Outside, in the bitterly cold, bitterly honest air.

That had been the first time he'd had the idea of setting out and finding Christ. He knew enough to know that the idea was a queer one, but he was young enough to accept it naturally, the way he accepted the snow and the woods and that sky that slowly burned itself into cinders before it turned dark. He decided at that moment on that afternoon of that Christmas Day that he would leave, would go, would risk all to find Christ. He made certain that his leather cap was on properly and that its flaps were fastened securely under his chin, he tightened his wool scarf about his neck, he smoothed the fingers of his well-worn gloves, he stomped his boots on the front walk that his father had shoveled clean an hour or so ago to make sure they fit snugly. And then he was ready. As he walked to the front gate, he took one last look over his shoulder at the frame house in which he'd lived since birth. Years before, he'd decided that it was ugly, cramped, and desolate: it held little or nothing for him except dreary memories and bad dreams. Its sole virtue resided in the fact that it was located on the outskirts of the town, so that beyond the wooden fence his father'd put up to enclose it lay the wide, beckoning, open world. The remote horizon, which was spun of infinite longing, and, somewhat nearer, the evergreen woods, which were the source of mystery …

It was in the distant, tantalizing woods (and the distance itself was tantalizing), that Alan thought to find Christ. He was sure Christ was there. There, living—no, the right word for what he wanted to say was *dwelling*—among the wonderful firs! Christ loved the dark, wild trees that burned like eternal green tapers against the wintry sky and refused to sputter out in rain or snow! Surely, Christ couldn't care for the other trees, those slashed down with ax and saw and draped with silly bulbs and frivolous ornaments! Christ had no use for murdered trees: it was the free, naked, living trees he cared for.

So, deep in the heart of those woods, Alan would find his Christ. What a joke! All the world was searching for Christ, was looking for him everywhere—and Alan would find him, out beyond the wooden fence, across the unspoiled snowdrifts, just before the far horizon that separated sky from earth, dwelling among the green-needled pines and yews and firs! Tate reached the gate and unlatched it and went through and was scrupulously careful to set the latch back in its place. There, that was it! Every move on his part was just so, just as it should be. Nobody could say that he'd been remiss or reprimand him. There, he was out! Out of the prison yard and into great, unbounded space. Already, he felt better. That was what finding Christ was all about.

His heart singing, he marched forward. He marched rapidly, with spirit. As he moved on, the wind beginning to sting his cheeks, he reached up and unfastened the button of the left breast pocket of his mackinaw; he fished out a nickel-plated compass and held it in front of him in the palm of his glove. He could see the woods and didn't need the compass, which he didn't actually know how to read, but that did not matter. It was good to have it before his eyes, like a guiding star. When he came upon Christ, he would be sure to show him the compass—for which he'd saved for almost a year. Perhaps he'd even give it to Christ as a gift.

"No," he thought as he strode over the fresh, seamless, sublimely smooth snow, holding his nickel-plated compass out in front of him like a divining rod and picking his way through the undulant drifts, "nobody has any notion of where to find Christ but I!" He pushed on. "And furthermore," he thought triumphantly, leaving boot tracks behind that the petulant wind began to obliterate almost the instant they were imprinted, "and furthermore, nobody has the faintest inkling of what Christ looks like—but I!" The paintings and the drawings were all wrong, of course. The pomaded hair and cornsilky beard and baby-blue eyes, and even the inescapable crown of thorns that could easily be confused with barbed wire! All of those notions were ridiculous—as garish and self-mocking as were Christmas trees! The plain fact was that he, though only a boy, knew what Christ really looked like—and it wasn't at all the way he was pictured in books and on posters and wall hangings and calendars.

According to Alan, Christ was a kind-of, sort-of combination lumberjack, forest ranger and Eagle Scout with every merit badge there was to earn. And what did he *do*? Well, he watched over campers and saw that no harm befell them when they were asleep in their pup tents; he was ever on the alert for violations and infractions of the law of the wild and kept strict order in the woods; he had a sharp eye peeled for brush fires, and stamped them dead in a jiffy with his two-inch thick rubber soles; he tended birds with broken wings and ministered to rabbits with injured feet and distributed food parcels to starving foxes and otters and muskrats; he outwitted poachers and drove malingerers away in panic; he healed the ailing trees and bound their wounds; he cleansed the streams and brooks and creeks of pollution; and he fought like a pride of lions against littering. He was strong, courageous, loyal, compassionate, dedicated, upright; he was fair and square, honest as the day is long. He was a no-nonsense, rough-and-tumble, never-say-die, always-keep-your-guard-up, heart-of-gold straight shooter who didn't know the meaning of the word "surrender" and who would not put up with chicanery, skullduggery, sleight of hand, or shenanigans! Oh, he was a shining silver dollar in a world of three-dollar bills!

That was, more or less, the way Alan as a boy had thought about Christ for a period of six months, perhaps as long as a whole year. Then he altered his view. He revised his vision—or maybe it revised itself. He couldn't say why; he hadn't a clue. It just happened. Like that. He woke up one morning and concluded that Christ was slimmer, not quite as tall as he'd pictured him, but even more muscular. Rather than bronze-toned, Christ's skin was ruddy-reddish. And he wore virtually no clothing at all, save for a simple, homespun loincloth. Except for that and the brush-thick, oiled and scented swath of jet-black hair that traversed his razor-shaven skull from forehead to the nape of his willowy neck, Christ was completely naked. On his magnificent, sinewy chest, depending from a necklace fashioned of bear's teeth, lay a multicolored talisman of beads, symbol of his majesty and regal authority; chains made of wild-cat claws adorned his well-turned ankles. Across one shoulder was slung a painted quiver filled with long, elegant, flint-headed arrows; a mighty, fire-cured bow slanted gracefully across the other …

This, divined Alan, was the true Christ! The real, honest-to-goodness Christ who hunted and fished with spear and knife blade and sling and bow, the Christ who snared fowl and trapped beasts. But these things Christ did only to meet his vital needs—never ever for sport and thrill or out of spite or malice. To him, the woods were as familiar as the palms of his very own hands. By instinct and by heart, he knew every path and hollow and stream and waterfall and cave, every knoll and cleft and dell.

Instantaneously, he picked up a trail and followed it hungrily, like a bloodhound of the spirit, straight from its starting point to the covert lair of the quarry. Possessed of infinite reserves of strength, he subsisted for days on end, consuming but a handful or two of dried maize and several swallows of brook water; he slept in utter repose on bare rock or in a thicket of nettles. For comradeship and help he counted on the star snails and sun peacock, on the whispering winds, the stuttering rains, the howling snows, and the ever revolving seasons; they gladdened and chastened and instructed and purified him. He could run thirty miles and walk a hundred and ride his trusty, dappled mount for three days and nights running without so much as pausing for a catnap. He heard the buffalo approaching a full twenty-four hours before they arrived; he smelled a brush fire burning beyond the mountains; he sensed death at the precise instant at which it occurred. He understood stones and bones and pebbles and plants and herbs and flame and rising smoke; he read the secret thoughts and inmost heart of man. He had an engaging smile, a disarming manner. But he also knew how to invoke black thunder and silver lightning. When his berry-red lips parted and he spoke, braves trembled and squaws wept copious tears and papooses hushed and wild creatures curled up at his toes and bounded unabashedly into his lap.

Christ, according to Alan, was not yet Chief, but as surely as the sun rose through the mists of dawn and slipped into the purple cloud reefs at eventide, he would one day be Chief. His position was staked out for him, ordained, decreed. Presently he sat in the circle of the Supreme Council in the most ancient wigwam of the territory and inhaled on the Pipe when it came to him, watching the smoke pass up and out the vent and scatter over the sky, as does the spirit of every creature when it dies, from thence to take its place in the Great Wheel of Creation. He mused; he discoursed; he asked and answered riddles; he drew inferences and analogies; he related parables; he advised and counseled and gave warning. He forecast the future, even his own demise, though it drew wails of anguish from his listeners.

And what he foretold did come to pass. Savant and sage, wise man and seer, proponent of justice and practitioner of mercy, lover of peace and relisher of life, Christ did become Chief. And, as he had also prophesied, he did meet his death. But he did not die as people later said he did. Not on any wooden crucifix, and not on any rusty cross. *Never.* No way. The truth, as Tate perceived it, was that Christ was charged with High Treason and taken from his federal dungeon and led to a lonely place littered with jackal dung and bound to a stake in front of the blue steel muzzles of a squad of United States cavalrymen just returned from slaughtering Apaches and shot at sunrise.

Thus did Christ die. And afterward, in the dead of night, whose merciful darkness would hide the shame of it, his subjects stole out to the execution ground and slashed the ropes that had held their beloved leader to the stake and took down the riddled corpse and brought it to the tribal burial grounds, there to tuck it neatly away in earth untrampled by animal hoof or cut by plowshare, down by the gurgling creek, not far from the place where the ponies were tethered. And there his subjects came to hurl themselves at his grave and mourn him.

But—

But it came to pass that he appeared again. Was seen again. Heard from again. Heard of again. There were rumors, stories, tales, reports, legends. There was whispering and talk and discussion and recounting. People sighted him. On the eastern ridges, silhouetted against the luminous wafer moon. Shooting the rapids of the mighty, foaming river in a canoe made of bark. Treading water on a steaming summer day in the glass-smooth water of a mountain-high lake. Trotting lickety-split down some half-forgotten trail on a saucy roan pony, his moccasined feet dragging lightly in the dirt. On the plains to the west, gliding effortlessly like a ghost toward the blood-red autumn sunset. People glimpsed him and passed the word. Men told their sons; women told their daughters; children playing beneath the giant sequoias murmured to each other.

That was Alan's version of what Christ's life was like for a number of childhood years. He stuck to it; it stuck to him like glue. It was only right for him to have formed it. Fitting and proper, since he'd loved the American Indians from the first moment he discovered them. They had a dignity that the White Man lacked, a reverence for life and respect for nature that seemed beyond the White Man's scope. They feared the invisible powers that the White Man mocked and derided; they cared for the land that the White Man raped and despoiled. In every Western film he saw, Alan clandestinely cheered the Indians and rooted for them to win, despite the fact that his hopes were perennially dashed to pieces. He dared not express his real feelings in public; it would have brought him only scorn and punishment.

Once, just once, for some desperate, inexplicable reason, forgetting who she was (and who he was in the bargain) he began—merely began—to tell his sister, Jennifer, about the Indians and about Christ. He stopped midsentence when he caught the look of shock and dismay in her hard eyes. Stopped midword and tried to switch the subject, talk about something—anything—else before it was too late. Alas, it was already too late. Jennifer turned on her heels and, like the bloodhound she loved to be, sought out and located their father. What she related to him exactly, Alan never knew. But the summons to appear before the Master of the House, relayed by his hollow-eyed wife, was not long in coming. Alan had to descend the steep, stone steps to the cellar, where the elder Tate had a combined wood and metal shop. The shop, which took up more than half of the damp basement and in which there was not a tool or implement out of place or a speck of dirt or grime anywhere to be seen, also served as a kind of court of familial justice. Alan's father would be seated on a high stool in front of a lathe on the work bench; the accused would face him and also the powerful light that beamed down from over the man's shoulder. Wearing a dark blue shop apron and a gray shirt whose sleeves were folded crisply to the elbow, Tate the senior straightened himself on the stool and ceremoniously cleared his throat. "Well, young man—" he began.

The phrase *young man* was a red alert, and Alan braced himself for the trouble that was certain to follow.

"I am given to understand," his father went on, clipping his words as if it cost him effort to part with them, "that, to all your other various and sundry flaws you have now added blasphemy! *Blasphemy*—" He repeated the word with grim emphasis. "By a son of mine!" He paused for a moment, glaring down at the accused. One of his large, thick-fingered hands rested on the blue metal of the lathe slightly behind him. The other massaged his chin with slow, even movements. "Now," he continued, "whether this blasphemy was some mindless eruption or whether it came as the result of devilish calculation makes not the slightest difference to me. The only point of importance is that I shall not tolerate it under my roof!" His voice had risen and his face darkened. The hand on his chin dropped with sudden impact and convulsed into a fist. "I shall not countenance blasphemy in this house! Ever! Have you understood, son? Has what I've said penetrated your skull? Or are you in need of a more drastic, physical warning?" Here, the fist uncoiled and the thumb hooked itself onto the belt of the shop apron, an obvious reference to the leather strap which he had on many occasions used to "beat some sense" into his son's head. "Well, young man, will you blaspheme again? *Will you?* Don't hang your head now, like a cur or a jackass. Speak up—answer me!"

Alan wasn't sure of the exact meaning of the word "blasphemy," but it clearly had to do with what he'd told Jennifer about Jesus Christ. Of that he was certain. He was also certain that he'd do precisely what he wanted to do and think exactly as he pleased, but he wasn't about to do battle with the Lord High Executioner on the Stool. Sometimes, in a certain situation, you had to submerge in order to surface elsewhere; you just needed enough breath to swim underwater. Coldly, he said: "I won't ..."

"Won't what?"

"Won't do ... what you said I did—"

"And what, pray tell, was that, young man?"

"Bias—"

The elder Tate nodded somberly. "Blaspheme—yes. You get my drift, do you not? You do know what I'm referring to?"

With stubborn coldness, Alan said, "Yes."

Again, his father nodded, this time gravely, with evident satisfaction. "Then we can consider our little interview concluded." His fingers tapped the polished lathe wheel. "You got off easily ... this time; you were lucky. But there'd better not be a next time."

Nothing further was required from the transgressor. Not one word. Not a syllable. Not the merest flicker of an eyelash. The trial was terminated. The verdict was in. The gavel had come down. And sentence had been passed. Now, the judge could lick his chops and the sinner his wounds. Tate was dismissed. He turned on his heels, just as his sibling had done, and took his leave.

At supper, his father boomed out grace like a cannoneer firing a salvo out over some rock-rimmed harbor and at once set about eating. The elder Tate shoveled in the corned beef and cabbage and boiled potatoes and home-baked bread as though these were the last portions of food to be had on earth; he washed it all down with great swills of his favorite ale. His wife ate sparingly, primly, even daintily, of the meal she had taken considerable pains to produce. Always on the verge of shudder or sigh, she kept her eyes cast down on her plate. And Jennifer smirked. She made no attempt whatsoever to hide the smirk. She brandished it greedily, like a pennant, in Alan's face. *Jennifer, the betrayer*, he thought. *Jennifer, the Judas!* She had slithered up to her father and turned her brother in. She had tattled, spilled the beans, squealed, ratted on him—and done it with malicious glee. Without a doubt, she'd been in the kitchen, at the doorway to the cellar steps, waiting for him to howl with pain and beg for mercy. Well, no such luck, Judas-girl! The Inquisition had given him a suspended sentence. But even if it had been different, even if he had been lashed with the thick, leather strap by the Man-with-the-Iron-Hand-and-Leaden-Heart, it still wouldn't have mattered a damn! Who cared what his father said or did to him? Long ago, he had cut the connection. Years before, even when he was very young, he had filled his lungs with pure, free air and submerged himself. What his father and mother and sister and all others beheld was merely a shell.

After supper, up in his cramped, deliberately sloppy attic room, with its steeply slanting roof and single window and half-eaten-away shutters, he burrowed through the endless stacks of books and piles of magazines and finally came up with his dog-eared, coverless dictionary. He sat on his rumpled bed and in the glare of the single bulb that hung from the ceiling flipped the pages until he found the word *blasphemy*. When he read the definition, he laughed aloud. His rigid, callous, tyrannical, hypocritical father the arbiter of what was or was not "impious"? He tossed the dictionary to the foot of his bed. What a bitter joke!

On that Christmas Day when he left the yard and set out for the distant woods, he thought back to the "blasphemy" incident. Though he needed none, though he was doing what he was doing for himself, it nevertheless gave him added impetus. He straightened his hat and banged his gloved hands together and increased his pace. Filaments of his whitened breath edged up into the freezing, dark air. His boots sank softly into the freshly fallen snow. The woods grew larger, but the day shriveled. By the time he reached his destination, dusk was coming on. In the flush of arrival, he failed to note it. Unable any longer to restrain himself to walking, he burst forward and trotted triumphantly into the welcoming embrace of the trees.

Officially, the woods were out of bounds, taboo. His father expressly forbade him to go there. "Too far and too dangerous," the elder Tate had said curtly. "And the subject is not open for further discussion." Of course, Alan disobeyed the prohibition. On any clear day, he could see the woods, gleaming like some magical garden, from his attic window, and they pulled at him with the force of some irresistible spiritual gravity. They seemed to promise him nothing less than infinity! So he'd gone to them. A number of times. Always surreptitiously. And always when his father wasn't in the house and wouldn't be back for a good while. But only once before in winter. And never during a period when there was snow. He'd explored them—up to the point where they plunged down a steep precipice and into a ravine. His favorite spot was a clearing with a large rock shelf that overlooked a pool formed in the course the creek took. Once, in summer, he'd taken tackle wound around a stick, a single hook and lead sinker, and worms he'd dug up in his backyard for bait and fished in the pool. He'd watched the iridescent rainbow trout, glittering more feverishly than any jewel he'd ever seen, wriggle toward the baited hook, and when they took it, he pulled them up. He caught five. But, for fear of being found out, he decided not to take them home. So he gave them away to the neighbor woman who never spoke a word of the incident to his father.

When he was younger, he believed that elves and gnomes and forest imps and assorted goblins lived in the woods. By the creek, there lived water nymphs with skin the color of pearl and breasts that had no nipples. But as he grew older, he became skeptical about such creatures and gradually discarded his belief in their existence; like fairy tales, they no longer seemed real to him. And then, late in the afternoon of a day during that very autumn, a day that blazed with bronze light like a newly minted coin, he saw as he sat by the window, resting an arm on the cracked sill and gazing dreamily out to the distance, the figure of an Indian brave, sitting erect on his saddleless mount and riding slowly toward the green woods. And it came to him at that instant that the rider was Christ! Christ, wearing a bonnet of eagle feathers and beaded moccasins that flashed like rainbow trout. Christ bearing his bow of gold and quiver filled with scarlet arrows! *But of course!* It was so simple, so clear, so right, so natural! What more appropriate and perfect place for Christ to live—that is, to dwell—than the woods of evergreen where the secret of life had first been propounded and was even now kept! His heart pounded; his eyes burned with tears that started from them like buds; he wanted desperately to cry out to Christ that he was there, at the attic window, and wanted to meet him—but he did not dare. His sister was bound to hear him and run blabbing to his father who would subpoena him to the basement, convict him of aggravated blasphemy and grind him into sawdust with the high-powered lathe! No, he couldn't possibly call out to Christ to come and get him. Instead, he would have to take himself to the woods and find Christ there.

On that waning Christmas Day, Alan headed straight for his private spot at the pool by the rock. Though little light was left, he was still able to pick out the various trail signs he'd left to lead him as directly as possible to the pool: grooves in the bark of trees, scraps of cloth suspended from low boughs, small piles of stones. Propelling himself swiftly through the snow-laden pine and fir needles, he headed straight for his goal—it didn't take him more than fifteen minutes to get there.

He halted. Stood stock still. In the final dregs of daylight that remained, he just barely made out the shape of the rock shelf; the pool below it was no more than a smudge of gray. The creek was frozen solid—more than likely, had been for more than a month—and there was no sound from it. Nor was Christ there. Nobody was there. Nothing was there. He was alone. He took a step forward and halted again. For a moment, he thought of going back, but he changed his mind almost as soon as he had the thought. Going back made no sense. He'd come all this way for a purpose, and the purpose had not altered; he wanted to find Christ. Christ wasn't there, but surely he had to return. The only thing to do was to stay there and wait for him.

Cautiously, he made his way across the clearing, spreading his arms and balancing himself as though he were on a tightrope high above some abyss. Usually, he jumped the creek, which was fairly narrow at this point, but now he could cross on the solid ice. He liked the glassy feel of the ice beneath his boots, and then he was across and on the far side. He groped his way to the rock, showering himself with snow powder from the branches. He dug his fingers into rock fissures and hoisted himself up. He brushed away a thin coating of snow and slowly seated himself.

The day was dead. Dead and buried, and it would never rise again. He had come to the burial place of the day; had come there to attend its funeral. He sat and looked around. He sat and watched as the clearing filled with mysterious darkness, just as though some invisible hand above were pouring black ink down into it. No longer could he delineate the trees that ringed him; he couldn't make out the gray smudge that had once been the pool or the faint swirl of charcoal that had marked the twisting course of the iced-over creek. Everything had turned black; he might as well have been blind. Leaning forward, he tugged his earflaps as far down as they went and rubbed the stiff palms of his gloves together and brought up his knees and lowered his numb chin into them. He shivered and said a little prayer for the day that had died.

When he finished, he looked up. Through the conical crests of the evergreens, he glimpsed the sky. It seemed to him to be as cold and as hard as the rock on which he sat. Here and there, a star that appeared to have been screwed into place glittered savagely. The wind soughed in the trees. Snow dust rippled down. The sound of the wind pained and bewildered him. It was a desolate song without words and without melody. He put his head to his knees. Where was Christ? When would he come? *Would he ever come at all?*

The last question disturbed him terribly. Maybe Christ had decided to pull up stakes and quit the woods and go to live in another place? Or maybe something had happened to him? Maybe his horse had thrown him and he was at this very instant lying somewhere in a snowdrift with a broken leg or arm or severed spine or barely conscious as a result of a concussion? Or maybe some White Man had spotted him and unslung his Winchester and knelt and sighted and blasted him point-blank for being off the Reservation or simply for being an Indian in the path of the Paleface Conquest? What if at that very instant Christ was stretched out face-down in the snow, his life's blood steaming as it gushed into the frosty air? Anything could have occurred. Christ could be in mortal need of his help, and here he was, anchored to a rock above a frozen pool and not doing a damn thing! He gritted his teeth and shifted position and swung his head on his stiffened neck and probed the darkness in all directions. Hopeless! Absolutely hopeless! How in the world was he supposed to know where to go? He felt impotent and depressed. And he was beginning to feel the cold.

He shivered. His body shook. Then he thought that he'd been unreasonable, silly. Why would Christ require his help? Christ was a big boy, and could certainly take care of himself. Man-devouring beasts and poisonous reptiles and hostile warriors from rival tribes and the perfidious White Man himself were less than fleas to Christ. No matter what the situation or who the enemy, he could more than handle himself. And, as for leaving these glorious, magical woods, who in his right mind would ever think of going elsewhere? No, he reflected, it was wasteful and perverse to think such ridiculous thoughts about Christ being in mortal danger or deserting the premises. What he had to do, he mused as his teeth chattered, was to wait patiently and pure-heartedly for Christ and to keep from freezing into a block of ice, if that were possible, while he waited.

Most assuredly, he would have frozen to death that night, had not one of the local outdoorsmen, also in love with the icicle-starred heavens and unbroken expanses of snow and dark, esoteric woods, happened by on some private pilgrimage and discovered him on the rock, lost in rapture and despair…

When Tate at length fell silent, Hadashi sighed. "The child Alan," he said slowly and so softly that he could scarcely be heard.

"The child Shmuel." He rose from his chair and stared down at Tate. A strange light shone in his eyes; he almost looked transfigured. *"The child pursues us all our lives long ..."* he whispered.

*   *   *

Hadashi slept in the big, back bedroom. Tate went to sleep in the living room, on the couch. He had just gotten the bedding from the closet and spread it out for the night when his companion, in pajamas and robe, his hair all tousled, came into the room. "Will you never go back to the States?" he asked.

"I think not," said Tate. "Why do you ask?"

"Simply to tell you that you are welcome to stay here with me as long as you wish. The thought struck me just now, and I wanted you to know."

"Thank you," said Tate, moved.

Hadashi smiled. "It's my great pleasure to have you here," he said. "You help me over the trail."

"What trail?"

"The trail of the past."

The next morning, after they'd finished breakfast, Hadashi brought out a violin case. "Ugh," he exclaimed, "but it's dusty! Wait just a moment. I'll get a cloth and clean it off." When he'd wiped it, the two of them sat down. Hadashi had the case on his lap; he opened it and carefully took out the instrument. In the soft light of the morning, the violin gleamed like a rose. "Isn't it a beauty?" he said. "Martha so loved to play and I to listen. We made a perfect team."

Tate looked at him. Hadashi's eyes were filled with both longing and the certain knowledge that it would never be satisfied. Then, quite inexplicably, his expression changed to one of amusement. "What is it?" Tate asked. "What are you thinking about?"

Hadashi chuckled. "Well," he said, "Martha once told me that if ever I were unfaithful to her, all the strings of this violin would snap—of their own accord, no less! My, but we had a good laugh over it!"

"Were you ever unfaithful?"

Hadashi seemed not at all taken aback by the question. "Unfaithful to whom?" he asked.

"Why, to your wife—to Martha—of course."

"I could never have been unfaithful to Martha," said Hadashi soberly, "only to myself—to my own commitment to the marriage." He gestured. "It's like theft, or other moral infractions: the violator is first of all unfaithful to himself. By his infidelity, he diminishes himself."

He put the violin back in its case.

* * *

So their life went forward—or as Hadashi remarked with a sly grin, they "pulled it forward, like a rickshaw." Through all of February, the weather was cold and rainy. The chill and the dampness penetrated the cinder block walls of the building. "Didn't they ever hear of such a thing as insulation?" Tate asked, shivering.

"They build mainly for the warm weather," Hadashi explained.

But he had a large, portable gas stove. It stood in the kitchen. He faced it toward the living room and kept it going for a great part of the time. Sitting comfortably in its warmth, they spent countless hours reading to each other aloud from their favorite books. Hadashi read often from the Bible in Hebrew, and Tate followed the English translation. "You know," said Tate one afternoon, "I'd like to learn some Hebrew."

"Are you serious?"

"Yes."

"Then I'll teach you."

"Wonderful!" exclaimed Tate. He hesitated. "Do you think I'll ever be able to read the Prophets and the Psalms in the original?"

Hadashi shrugged. "That depends on you," he said. "And on me. And … on the rickshaw …"

They set a regular time for the lessons: after supper. The place was at the kitchen table. They sat opposite each other. The gas stove burned, all four of its rectangular stones glowing. Often, as they studied, rain spattered the windows and the wind rattled the panes. One night, Tate was edgy. Hadashi picked it up immediately. "What's the matter, Alan?"

"My progress leaves much to be desired, no?"

Hadashi shook a finger. "I'm afraid you've got it backward," he said. "What you really mean to say is that you devoutly desire progress!"

* * *

March came. At best, an unstable month. At worst, a wild one. Some days, violent storms made them shut-ins; other days, they could go out. Making their way one morning from Dizengoff Circle, where they'd watched the fountain spit water and fire, down Bograshoff (Hadashi had once told Tate that the street was named for the American actor, Humphrey Bograshoff!) to the sea, they were caught in a sudden rain. Not an easy rain—a torrential downpour. Oddly enough, as so often happens in life, they hadn't even noticed the gathering clouds. But there it was: a blanket of rain as thick and gray as a prison wall. Quickly, they ducked under an awning. "Just in the nick of time," sputtered Hadashi.

He was right. The rain turned to hail. Pea-sized clots of frozen rain pelted the sidewalks and street. It drummed on the awning and clacked over the pavements. Tate noticed that they were standing in the entrance to a clothing store. Through the show window, he saw mannequins. They stared back at him with marble eyes, and he averted his eyes to the street where cars were creeping by with their headlights on. The hail persisted for about five minutes and then switched back to rain. A downpour. A flood. The sidewalks streamed. Sewers backed up. And then the rain was gone. Holding out a hand, Tate said: "It's stopped. We can go on."

They walked toward the sea. Hadashi, who had been silent all the while, looked over at his companion. "You know," he said, "you appear before God naked and wanting. You stick out your hand like the beggar you are. God nods, and from His sack dumps sand into your open palm. The sand is *time*. At once, you close your fingers. Hard. You make the tightest fist you can. Of course, it doesn't help you. The sand trickles through—no matter what you do, how much you try. And in the end, you've nothing left. Not a single grain of sand. But you cannot go back to God for more. Not even one speck. That's the way you must play His game."

*   *   *

Gray-blue cloud cliffs reared up at the horizon to the west. Waving cheery white handkerchiefs, the waves smashed their heads on the breakwaters; oceanfront palms bowed respectfully to the wind. In the distance, way down to the south, Jaffa rose gracefully from the compost heap of dead centuries like some phantom city. The two of them walked side by side along the promenade, drawing deep breaths; Tate held fast to the peak of his cap; Hadashi slashed the air with his cane. On sudden impulse, he cried out—partly to his companion, partly to the world, but mostly to himself: *"I'm young! I'm reborn! It's all ahead of me! All of it!"*

Tate didn't comment. But he knew what Hadashi meant. The clouds. The sea. The trees. The day itself. All were beautiful. Exhilarating. It was what lurked behind them that bothered him. What lurked behind his own eyeballs. "'I've 'scotched the snake,'" he thought suddenly, "'not—'" But he didn't finish the line.

On the left, across Herbert Samuel Boulevard, were several restaurants in a row. "If we tried," Hadashi ventured, "I wager we could eat in every restaurant in Tel Aviv. Think so—?"

Tate shrugged. He had no answer. Not even an opinion. The day pained him. He was making an effort to avoid the open pit of his wound, and it took all his energy.

"Hungry? Want to eat now?"

Tate shook his head. "No, no. Let's walk."

Walking helped. So they walked. To the left, beyond the boulevard and Hakov'shim Street were the narrow streets and Casbahlike houses of the Kerem-Hateimanim—the so-called Yemenite Quarter—and the adjacent shuk. They kept on walking. All the way down to the end of the promenade, almost to the old Dolphinarium. Just ahead of them were the Dan Panorama and the Textile Center. Jaffa lay beyond. "Well," said Hadashi, taking his friend's arm, "shall we follow the yellow brick road?"

"How do you know that?" asked Tate.

Hadashi's eyes lit up. "Martha and I saw the film. A long time ago, when we lived in Jerusalem. We took Carmi. He was just a child, then."

They got as far as the IZL Museum, but didn't continue on to Jaffa. Hadashi tired, so they caught the Number 10 bus back to the center of the city. "Sorry," Hadashi apologized.

"Some other time," said Tate.

"If the sand hasn't run out of our fists."

* * *

That night, Hadashi was ill. He assured Tate that it was nothing serious, nothing to worry about.

"Something you ate?" Tate suggested. "That spicy Indian food?"

"No, no," said Hadashi. "I took my temperature. I have a little fever. It's a flu, I think."

Tate boiled a kettle of hot water and made him tea with lemon.

"Three cubes of sugar, please," said Hadashi.

"I know," said Tate with a smile.

After he'd drunk three cups, Hadashi took a couple of aspirins and went to bed. "Don't fret," he said. "I'll be better in the morning."

That was about eight.

So Tate had the entire night to himself—the first he'd had since Hadashi signed for his release from the hospital and he'd come to live with his benefactor on Vitkin Street. He was somewhat anxious. Why? The strange pain he'd experienced during the day was one factor. "And then I'm new at being on my own," he told himself. That seemed to settle things. To quiet him. He got the Hebrew textbook Hadashi had picked for him, his notebook, and a pen and went into the kitchen. It felt queer sitting at the table alone. But there was no choice. He concentrated on his work.

Hadashi had given him the assignment the night before, and he went over it now. He had twenty vocabulary words to memorize; he made certain he knew them. Then there were four verbs to conjugate in the simple and intensive moods; he reviewed that as well. Lastly, he had to use the words and verbs in sentences. He checked what he'd done and then began to read ahead in the textbook. Hadashi would be pleasantly surprised.

Hardest for Tate had been learning the Hebrew alphabet. But he had made an enormous effort and mastered it completely. "Now you're really on your way!" Hadashi had told him. "So I am!" Tate responded triumphantly. And he was. Soon he was able to make elementary conversation and decipher signs in the street. "My grand aim," he told his teacher over and over, "is to reach the cloud-piercing pinnacles of the Bible" (Hadashi had thought what he said poetic). But that seemed remote. "Like the prophet, Moses," said Tate, "I'll probably die before I get there."

"Who knows?" laughed Hadashi.

But his eyes were serious.

* * *

It took Tate about an hour and a half to finish his homework. He felt satisfied. Even optimistic. Perhaps one day he would achieve his goal, after all. He closed his books but did not get up to put them away. Instead, he sat where he was, listening to the rain. Had it been dry, he might have gone out to a film or a concert, as he and Hadashi sometimes did. Beginning to feel restless again, he went into the living room and turned on the TV. Backed by a band, a female singer was emptying her lungs, which might just as well have been bellows. He was about to switch the channel when a special news bulletin came on. He stiffened as he watched. *A lonely West Bank road. Blue lights flashing. Border policemen milling around. Soldiers in bulletproof vests. The rear doors of an ambulance bumping away. Off-camera, a hovering helicopter that at times drowned out the voice of the reporter. At the side of the road, half-buried in weeds, the gutted remains of a car. And farther down, surrounded by settlers with weapons, a middle-aged man with a soot-smeared face grasping the hand of a weeping child. The camera wobbled over the scene; it moved in on the group of people. But when the reporter tried to approach, he was shoved back by the settlers.*

Suddenly, Tate turned. Hadashi was standing behind the chair, watching. "How do you feel?" Tate asked.

"A little better, thank you."

"How long have you been standing here?"

"I saw it all."

"What exactly happened?"

"It was a terrorist strike. In Samaria. The car was going east from the city of Ra'anana to a settlement. Arabs threw a firebomb, and the car caught fire. The man and the little boy managed to get out. But the man's wife and daughter were burned ..."

"Burned? Will they be all right?"

"No," said Hadashi. "They were burned to death. The little girl was two."

Tate was silent.

"It doesn't end," said Hadashi: "It just doesn't end."

Tate remained silent.

"Better not to watch the news—"

Tate cleared his throat. "But what are you doing up? You're supposed to be sleeping—"

The other shrugged. "I went to the bathroom. Then I heard the damn TV." He turned. "I'm going back to bed now. See you in the morning."

Tate sat where he was. Didn't stir. Didn't think. Breathed, because he had to. On the TV screen, image flashed after image. He made no sense of them. He clicked the set off. The apartment was dead silent. He no longer heard the rain—it must have stopped. There wasn't a sound. Sound must have disappeared from the world. Except—

Except for the maniacal ticking of Hadashi's grandfather clock. Tate found it annoying. Exasperating. Infuriating. It seemed to mock him, to goad him, to challenge him. But to what? Why was it necessary? Why did there have to be a clock ticking in the scheme of things? He squirmed in his chair. He gritted his teeth. He stood it as long as he could. Then he got up out of the chair and went directly over to the clock. Stood in front of it. Confronted it. Eyeball to eyeball. There was a little silver-plated key in the lock of the clock's glass door. He could turn it and open the door and stop the pendulum. That would take care of the ticking! That would teach the clock a lesson! He actually reached for the key. But then he pulled back his hand. *He was afraid. Afraid that in the morning, the clock would tell Hadashi what he'd done.*

* * *

Tate lay on the couch, his back toward the window. Toward the rain that no longer fell. He didn't properly know if he was awake or asleep, but he knew he heard the clock. *"Save me! Save me! Save me!"* That was what it said. *"Save me!"* But then how could it be the clock? Clocks didn't talk. Even though he'd feared that the clock might snitch on him to Hadashi if he were to arrest the pendulum, he really knew that clocks couldn't speak. They ticked and chimed and sounded alarms, but they never tattled. Yet he kept hearing the cry. *"Save me!"* Surely, it wasn't the clock. Who, then? Someone he knew? A stranger? The woman and child who'd been burned alive in the car? Or—himself? But what did he want to be saved from? He didn't know. Didn't want to find out. Now, all he wanted was to sleep. To pull the dark blanket of sleep over his mind. To forget—*to forget what he did not dare to remember.*

* * *

The next morning, Hadashi seemed somewhat better. He was still a little pale and drawn, but his fever had gone. "Gone back to wherever fevers come from," he said with a wry smile. He drank his grapefruit juice and reached for a seeded roll. "Well, I've an appetite," he said. "That's promising."After breakfast, brushing crumbs from his robe, he said: "Alan, have you peeked out the window? Did you see? A day like the first day God ever created! We can't possibly ignore it. Let's get dressed and go out!"

"Are you certain you're well enough?" asked Tate.

"The day will make me well, Alan! Now, get a move on! We're late as it is." Hadashi looked at his companion. "You look a bit pale yourself, Alan. I hope you didn't catch anything from me."

"No, no," said Tate. "I didn't sleep very well, that's all."

"Save me!" said the clock.

Only Tate heard it.

Tel Aviv, March 11, 1993
Kikar HaMedinah Plaza
12:10 pm

They varied their regular itinerary. Instead of the promenade and the sea, they went in the opposite direction, crossing Ben Yehuda and Dizengoff and then heading north toward Kikar Hamedinah. Hadashi was right about the day. It was if winter had fallen from its perch and spring seized the reins. Fleecy clouds drifted across the sky. There were birds in the trees and cats on the lawns, sunning themselves. Some of the shrubs were budding. The air seemed washed. And the sun was so warm that the two men unbuttoned their coats.

They had a light lunch outside at a cafe on Jabotinsky Street, just off the circle, and then started back. "How about the sea, now?" asked Hadashi.

"Are you up to it?"

"Are you kidding?" Hadashi said. He swung his cane.

They headed south, cutting over to Ben Gurion Boulevard and then to Gordon Street, where they stopped from time to time to look at the paintings in the windows of the galleries. When they got to the promenade, it was just past three. They walked for a while and then seated themselves on a bench. The sea shone placidly; it seemed to have given up its anger. There were a few sun bathers on the beach and even several people in the water. Tate glanced over at his friend. Hadashi had color in his cheeks; he looked relaxed. It was a pity that his cane had tapped *"Save me!"* on the sidewalks.

*　　*　　*

Hadashi hadn't spoken in some time. He had closed his eyes—maybe he had dozed off? "Shmuel," Tate said softly. He would never call his companion "Shmuelik" or "Shmuelkeh," as neighbors and acquaintances and the local storekeepers did—only "Shmuel," just as he wished always to be called "Alan."

"Shmuel," he said once again. "Are you asleep?"

Hadashi didn't answer. He sat hunched over, head fallen forward to chest, hands folded peacefully on his lap, cane propped up against the bench. He looked like a statue set out in a garden, waiting to be covered with lichen and moss. Tate was relieved. He cared for Hadashi and knew that Hadashi cared for him. But still Tate was relieved. Glad to be alone. He *needed* to be alone. Since the scenes of the firebombing on TV, something had happened to him. His center of gravity had shifted. *He was on the brink—*

His head was turned slightly to the right. Out of the corner of his eye, he saw a foursome strolling slowly down the boardwalk. A family. On an outing. He in a black and white *kaffiyah* and loud business suit, his wife in a *yashmak* and gaudy dress. The children—a boy of about ten and a little girl of about three—held hands as they walked. They came closer. Closer and closer. Not afraid to promenade in Tel Aviv. No fear of firebombs. Safe among the Jews. But if the situation were reversed? If a Jew or gentile Westerner were to go for a walk in Jenin or Kalkilya or Hebron or Gaza? What then? Tate knew the answer. Oh, it was a grim answer! And Tate knew it so well—

He rose.

There was that fatal split second. That seesaw instant on which his life balanced. In which it might have gone up or down. And then it was decided. Signed. Sealed. Yet to be delivered. Tate looked down at his companion and friend and benefactor, at the man who pitied and had empathy, at the man who'd helped him leave the hospital and had taken him into his own home and own life. But also the man who had not understood him, had not really grasped what had happened inside him, what was happening now. Tate sighed. Hadashi was indeed sleeping. The moss was indeed gathering. One could see it on the slope of the shoulders, in the heavy folds of the face. "Good-bye, my dear friend," Tate whispered: "It—what you hoped for and wanted so badly—just isn't possible for me. I have my own destiny to embroider. *I, the needle … and I, the cloth …*"

He stretched out a hand that Hadashi would never take.

*   *   *

Tate turned toward the approaching Arabs. He heard the guttural speech of the parents—they sounded as if they had jagged pieces of tin can in their throats. The children had merriment in their eyes; they laughed. The parents exchanged glances of pleasure. At their leisure, they'd walk, talk, gaze at the ocean, watch the gulls and the kites. Have *shishlik* and chips and tea with *nana*. The kids'd have popcorn and coke. Use the public rest rooms if they had to. Whatever they wanted. At their ease. Why not? Tel Aviv was their oyster. Tate walked swiftly to meet them. Saw a charred car. A shell-shocked man. A weeping child. A rock snarling through space. Heard the crunch of stone on skull. Ground his teeth. Reached for his knife. Except—

Except that it wasn't there!

He didn't understand. The knife in its sheath should have been in place. Snug on his thigh, where he'd put it. He groaned aloud. He groped, knowing it was in vain. The Arabs were passing, filling the air with the splinters of their speech. *So close.* The woman with her thick-painted lips and jumbo earrings; the husband in his green, double-breasted suit, with floral tie and diamond pinky ring. *Where was Tate's knife? Why had it been taken from him?* His mind was high again. On a trapeze, swinging high above the dismal circus of the world. *How could he come down as steel when he had no knife?* He had been robbed. He had been castrated.

The Arab family passed him by. He watched them go. They shrank down the boardwalk. Pygmies. Dolls. Flyspecks. Lost.

So was he.

* * *

He was found.

Hallelujah!

He had found himself.

Hosannah!

He was in Jerusalem, City of Holiness.

Hosannah in excelsis!

But how had he come to be in Jerusalem?

Yet why did it matter, as long as he was there?

He looked around. Jerusalem was familiar to him—as familiar as his most intimate memories, as familiar as the texture of his dreams, and yet it was alien, as if he'd never been there before. For one thing, the light was most peculiar. It seemed to reach the buildings and the streets as through a filter. And then the people, the passersby, the pedestrians—they were another thing. The people moved in slow motion, bouncing up and down and seeming almost to float, as in some film sequence where the director wishes to show that life has somehow been wrenched out of place—"although," as Tate thought, "where is the place that life should be?"

So there he was, in the strangeness but also in settings that were known to him. Places saturated with the emotions that he attached to them, places where he'd been and thought and felt and lived. Only they were all mixed up, jumbled together, as if he viewed them through a kaleidoscope. The hotel, Binyanei-Haooma, the Ben-Yehuda mall, Independence Park, the Tower of David Museum, Hillel Street, the Shrine of the Book, Agrippa, the cafe on Neve'im Street, the Jaffa gate: all of them wrapped together like a system of entrails.

What did he want in Jerusalem? That was the real question. Once he knew that, everything would be hunky-dory, A-OK. In the meantime, he drifted. Just drifted. Like a feather. Like a tumbleweed, eased on by the wind. Down the length of Jaffa Road, in the direction of the Old City. At Zion Square, he halted. Something had clicked. Hillel Street. *Of course!* He wanted Hillel Street and the camping goods store. That's why he had come to the holy city of Jerusalem. He turned to the right. Hillel Street should have been just ahead, but it wasn't. He seemed to be in an alley. There was no one around, except for a beggar in rags crouching in a doorway.

The beggar held out a filthy hand. "Alms," he cried out. "For the love of man, alms—"

"All right," said Tate. "I heard you the first time." He reached into one pocket and then into the other. "I'm sorry," he said, "but I don't have any money. Not a red cent." He stared at the beggar. "You don't believe me, do you?"

"I believe you," said the beggar.

But Tate turned the pockets inside out. "See," he exclaimed. "See—they're completely empty! I've no money at all. It—it's all in Margie's change purse …"

The beggar shrugged. "Thank you for the good intent," he said.

But Tate didn't leave. Suddenly, he struck his forehead with the palm of his hand. "What the deuce is the matter with me?" he cried out. "It's that damn forgetfulness again! Of course I have money! It's in my wallet. It was there all the time. How ridiculous—" He fished for his wallet and took out a hundred-dollar bill—one of those that Margie'd set aside for a house present. "Here," he said, "take it—"

His eyes met the beggar's eyes.

"Here—" Tate repeated.

But the beggar pushed Tate's hand aside.

"What's the matter?" said Tate.

"Please," said the beggar, *"don't give me anything. You are more in need than I …"*

*   *   *

Maybe he'd made a wrong turn? Or turned too soon? Maybe that was why he couldn't find Hillel Street and the store with all the knives? He changed his direction and headed back toward Jaffa Road. He had to hurry. Suppose other people came to buy the knives? Suppose by the time he got there, there was none left? What would he do then? He quickened his pace, broke into a trot. The alley seemed to have no end.

He never reached Jaffa Road. Instead—in some violent shake of the kaleidoscope—he found himself at the *Kotel.* He couldn't believe it. He thought to rub his eyes, but there was no need: it was true. A lot of unbelievable things were true—he'd come to find that out lately. So he was there. Standing in front of the great, flagstoned plaza and the divider between the men's and women's sections and—

He stopped dead in his tracks.

Something incredible had come to pass!

The wall that he had seen and touched and known as the Western Wall was now part and parcel of a huge, soaring edifice whose stones seemed to radiate light from some source within them. The light blinded him—yet it soothed his eyes. He stared wildly. He broke out in a sweat. *It could not be—and yet it was!* The Temple was rebuilt. The Third Temple was reconstructed. The Third Temple of Zion! *For real.*

He fell to his knees. "Oh, Lord ..." He murmured. Then he lifted his eyes. "Oh, God!" he cried out. "Oh, God of wonders, You've done it! You've rebuilt it! You've raised Your Temple anew!"

And God's voice said: "Arise, Al—"

"Alan," said Tate. "Please call me Alan. I hate Al."

"Arise, O my son, Alan, and enter—"

The custodian waited at the wrought-iron gate to the plaza. He wore the same bedraggled clothes and the same misshapen, undersized cap, except that now a silver-plated Star of David—which Tate thought looked exactly like an Old West sheriff's badge—was pinned crookedly to it. The little man pulled a cardboard skullcap from a crate and handed it to Tate.

"Thank you," said Tate, placing it on his head.

The custodian smiled. "Compliments of the House of David," he said. Then he pointed ahead.

In front of a small door on whose polished redwood panels were carved the emblems of the Twelve Tribes of Israel, the gatekeeper was waiting expectantly. He wore a brocaded robe and a queer, six-pointed hat and looked remarkably like the Parisian reception clerk at the Hilton Hotel. "Mr. Tate," he said in a tremulous voice.

"Yes, I'm Alan Tate."

"Please excuse the fact that you're entering by the side door," he confided, "but we wished to make this as inconspicuous as possible. To avoid the media, you know."

"It's perfectly all right with me."

The gatekeeper inclined his head. "Do come in, Mr. Tate. This way. Right this way, please."

The gatekeeper carried a torch and led the way, Tate following close behind. Footsteps echoing, they made their way down marble and wood-paneled corridors (Tate recognized it as genuine cedar wood, brought from the mountain slopes of Lebanon) until they reached the arched entranceway to an enormous hall. Tate blinked. The hall was lit by a thousand tapers and hung with velvet drapes the size of a schooner's sails. Tate touched the gatekeeper's shoulder. "What is this place?" he asked.

"We have services and ceremonies and feasts in here," said the gatekeeper. He steadied the torch. "And sometimes weddings and bar mitzvahs. But never funerals. It's a policy of management."

Then Tate saw the vast, waiting throng. "And who are they?" he asked.

The gatekeeper waved his free hand. "Everybody," he said. "Everybody's here."

There was a stir in the crowd, and two people, a man and woman, emerged. The man wore a white tuxedo with matching white skullcap, and the woman a blue prom dress and rhinestone tiara. They looked up at Tate. The man bowed slightly from the waist; the woman curtsied.

"Who are they?" said Tate.

"The king and queen of Israel," replied the gatekeeper.

"King and queen?"

The gatekeeper nodded. "The monarchy has been restored. You remember—the seed of Jesse and so forth."

"But the tiara's rhinestone."

"Budget," said the gatekeeper crisply. "The country's on an austerity budget." He lowered his voice. "Long overdue, if you ask my opinion."

Then trumpet peals rang out, their notes springing giddily back and forth across the vast chamber like ten thousand iridescent Ping-Pong balls and the king and queen retreated and the crowd fell back and parted like the Red Sea dividing and Tate beheld a great, oaken table covered with a lace cloth as white as the wings of doves and resplendent with heirloom china and vintage silver service. And by the table stood waiters and butlers and maidservants and handmaidens and footmen and charboys and chimneysweeps and valets, should the help of any be required.

And Tate said, "What is this table?"

And God's voice said: "O my son, Alan, it is for you. Approach."

And when Tate drew near unto the table, he saw that eleven of its places were occupied: only the twelfth chair, at the head, was empty. And he came still nearer, and he saw who had been summoned to dine there.

At the foot of the table—Tate sensed that it was Judas's place—sat Tate's own father, holding on to his engraved dinner invitation tightly and looking smug. When he caught sight of his son, he attempted to hide his annoyance. "What are you doing here, Al?"

Tate bit his lip. "Alan," he said. "I've told you a thousand times."

"Alan—Al—Alan! What's the big deal? Your name won't change your personality—or your fate." He gestured. "This here meal's reserved, you know. It's not for ... everyone."

"I've been invited," said Tate.

"Oh? Who invited you?"

"The Boss," said Tate.

The elder Tate shook his head. "Must be a mistake."

To his father's right, Tate saw Jennifer, in a black mantilla and lace-trimmed matching gown. She flicked a fan fashioned of raven feathers in front of her mouth to hide the smirk. She said not a word, and her brother returned the compliment.

Next came Tate's mother. She was clad in calico and had the letter R embroidered in Christmas colors on her bonnet. "It's for Rebecca of Sunnybrook Farm," she told Tate and lowered her eyes.

"We should talk," said Tate.

"I ran out of talk years ago."

"Mother—"

"I ran out of mothering years ago, as well."

"We may not have another chance—"

But his mother turned her head away.

The next three chairs were occupied by American Indians, naked except for feathers, war paint and loincloths. They looked like store mannequins and had marble eyes that registered nothing. "Still," Tate thought, "they're here."

On his father's left, Tate saw Carey, his army buddy, from the time of the Texas POW camp. Carey wore his WW II khakis and on his head a soda jerk's cap instead of a military hat. Above the pocket of his shirt was pinned a single campaign ribbon, the color of blood. "You get it for dying," he told Tate. "Though, to tell the truth, I don't understand. Living's the hardest campaign." And he smiled his soft, old Carey grin—the one he'd carried modestly into the Kingdom of Darkness.

Then came another young man, also in an army uniform, but not American. A red beret was tucked under the strap on his shoulder; paratrooper wings were fastened to his chest. "When I jumped out of the plane, I landed on the Other Side," he said. And was still. Tate looked puzzled, and he spoke again. "My name's Carmi," he said: "Hadashi's dead son. Don't you recognize me from the photographs?"

The woman sitting next to him wore a high-necked blouse fastened shut with a brooch and had her glossy, auburn hair tied back in a bun. Without waiting for Tate to speak, she said: "And I'm Martha. You remember—Hadashi's wife." She held up a violin. "This is my new instrument. It's a genuine, certified Heavenly Fiddle. God Himself gave it to me. 'For keeps,' He said. But I won't be able to play anything now. I wasn't booked for this particular affair."

Tate nodded and turned his attention to the person on her left. His heart stopped.

It was—

Yes, it was—

"Sarah!" he cried out in anguish and exultation: *"Sarah, my darling!"*

A strong arm stayed him.

"Please," he implored. "You don't understand. It's my daughter—"

The gatekeeper had vanished. In his stead, was an archangel with six fiery wings. Michael—Raphael—Uriel—Gabriel. Tate could not tell which. Nor did it matter!

"Please," he begged. "She's my daughter, Sarah. She was killed in a car accident. I haven't seen her in years."

"Not yet," said the archangel.

Tate wept.

And God's voice said: "Al—"

"Alan—oh, Lord, *Alan*. Forgive me, but I really can't stand Al."

"I'm sorry, Alan. I forgot again. I don't know what's wrong with Me these days."

"You're too busy, maybe. Too preoccupied. Too pressured. Too—"

"Self-absorbed," said God's voice. "That's what it must be."

"Oh, God, please let me be near my daughter. Let me embrace Sarah. I beg of You."

"All in good time, Alan. You'll embrace your daughter, Alan. And your wife, Margie, as well."

"She's here? *Margie's—here?"*

Then Tate caught sight of her. She was sitting on Sarah's left, next to the empty chair at the head of the table. *He could really see her!* She was wearing her light-blue dress, the one she'd died in. *She waved.* "Oh, God," Tate cried out as he lunged forward. "This is too much."

But the archangel held him fast. "Didn't you hear what God told you?"

"It's—so hard!" Tate sobbed.

The archangel had twisted Tate's head, and he had a fleeting glimpse of the throng again. It was no more than a blur. Here and there, a general's or admiral's or field marshal's gold epaulets glinted, or a count's or duke's or earl's ivory-crested buttons winked, or a talk-show host's capped teeth gleamed like an ear of baby corn. And then—as if a light bulb had popped—it all went out.

The hall plunged into darkness. Then, as if footlights had suddenly been snapped on, the table and diners reappeared. The effect was startling. It looked to Tate like a tableaux, like a freeze-frame in a film—almost like an oil painting. Michaelangelo might have done it. Or Da Vinci. Or perhaps Van Gogh?

And God's voice said, "Alan—you see, I did remember this time—do you know what this is?"

And Tate said, "Yes, Lord. It's a dinner party. But there won't be any music. Martha—that's Hadashi's wife—told me so."

And God's voice said, "It's a very special dinner party, Alan. Look again. Tell me what it is."

And Tate looked again. "Why, it's the Last Supper."

And God's voice said, "Yes, my son. It surely is the Last Supper."

And Tate said, "But, where is he?"

"Is who?"

Tate was surprised. "Why, the man who's supposed to be sitting at the head of the table."

"You mean Jesus?"

"Yes, Lord. Where is Christ?"

And God said, in a voice that made the floor quake, "The place at the head of the table is for *you*."

"For me?"

"Yes, my son. You are the anointed one, the chosen one, the savior of the Jews and of mankind. *Messiah!* Go forward, Alan. Sit down. Eat. Enjoy. Enjoy the Last Supper. There won't be any more."

"All right," said Tate. "All right. I accept the invitation. But before I sit down—I beg of you, oh Lord—let me be with my wife and my daughter. I want to hug and kiss my dear Sarah. I want to hold Margie in my arms again and dance with her. In slow motion, maybe, they way they do in the movies when they're in love. Let Martha play, Lord. And give me one last dance with my wife."

And God said, in a voice that could create or destroy a world, "As you wish, my son. So it shall be done."

And the vast throng of onlookers that had been a blur became a shadow and then the shadow of a shadow and then was gone. And there was music—strings and woodwinds and horns—the works. And the archangel left off restraining Tate. As God had instructed, he moved forward.

Flash bulbs popped. TV cameras whirred like insects. Shutters clicked. A mob of reporters surged forward, jostling each other for position, until the archangel raised his flaming sword. But they called out to him:

"Tate—"

"Mr. Tate—"

"How does it feel—?"

"Give us a statement—"

"Mr. Tate—"

"Tate—"

Tate ignored them, ignored everything except his wife and his daughter. He was close. So very close. "Margie!" he sobbed. "Sarah! Come to me. Both of you. Oh, how I've missed you!"

He opened his arms—

And—*poof!*—the table and the chairs and the diners and the attendants and the reporters and the archangel and the hall and the resurrected Temple and the plaza and Jerusalem and the world and the stars and planets and novas and nebulae and galaxies and solar systems and the universe and time into which the universe was born—

And Tate. Alan Tate. Oh, yes, Tate. His joys, his sorrows. His hopes, his fears. His body, his mind. Sarah, emerging from the lake, laughing shrilly, her face and neck and shoulders spotted with shining beads of water; Margie, sitting at sunset on the window sill of the attic room of the farmhouse; the little boy on the rock in the dark, freezing woods, waiting for Christ or oblivion, whichever came first—

His life; even his death—

All … all of it vanished.

Like a puff of smoke from an opium pipe!

* * *

The kite was high. So very high that he thought it might bump into the invisible stars—or even the planets. He was sure that it had never been so high before, even when Amatzia was with him. Amatzia was his older brother. The kite danced in the air. It bobbed; it leapt; it soared.

The boy who stood on the beach and held the kite's string was copper-skinned, curly-haired, and had just last week turned twelve. His name was Yirachmiel Hacohen. He was a Yemenite. He lived in a third-floor apartment on nearby Ezra Hasofer Street, and he had built the kite with Amatzia. Yirachmiel was so delighted with the kite and absorbed in its stunning performance that he failed to notice the man in the leather jacket and tan golfer's cap descend the concrete ramp from the promenade above and head across the sand toward the sea.

Head thrown back, red lips parted, Yirachmiel tracked the astonishing antics of his creation. The kite was so very far above the earth—just a small patch of brilliant colors tugging its way toward heaven. The boy cheered and urged the kite on. He never once saw the man in the jacket and cap tramp through the sand and, fully dressed, step into the foaming surf. He never saw the man's shoes and trouser cuffs get soaked, the waves strike his calves and thighs. He was too busy.

Suddenly, without warning, something happened. Yirachmiel never knew what it was: maybe a lack of wind, or a savage gust of air, or perhaps some devious current. The kite began to buck. He struggled with the string to keep control. But the kite veered in one direction and then in the opposite. It dipped; it swooped; it made vicious loops; it slipped and it slid, all the time coming closer to earth. The boy pulled and yanked; he ran headlong with the string; he reversed field: he did everything his older brother, Amatzia, had taught him; he did everything he possibly could. But the kite was coming down.

Down from the heights. Down from sky. With furious speed. Down and down and down, slashing through the air like a knife blade. The boy made frantic, last-ditch efforts. But he knew they were doomed to failure. The kite had made up its mind. When it crashed, Yirachmiel cried out. He was hurt for himself and for Amatzia; he was hurt for the kite. He knelt in the sand to inspect the wreckage. The cross-bar had splintered, and the paper ripped to shreds. It was at that very instant that he caught sight of the man standing chest-high in the sea and moving outward. The boy stood up.

He stared in disbelief as the man went deeper. Stepping forward, Yirachmiel called out: "Hey you! Don't go swimming there! It's not allowed! Do you hear me? *Hey, mister—*"

But the man went deeper. Now, he was up to his shoulders. And then the boy realized that the man never meant to swim. Yirachmiel turned and raced for the boardwalk. "Help!" he screamed. "Help!" He cupped his hands to his mouth. *"Help!"* he screamed. *"There's a man out there—"*

He kept calling. But nobody heard him. Nobody came.

In despair, out of breath, he faced to the sea again. Far out, there was a speck—as tiny in the water as the kite had been in the sky. He could not tell whether the speck was rising or falling, whether it was man or angel. And then, blinded by the power of the sun, he could tell nothing at all.

OTHER BOOKS BY CHAYYM ZELDIS

Novels:

BROTHERS (Random House, The Toby Press)

THE BROTHEL (G.P. Putnam)

GOLGOTHA (Avon Books, Futura)

THE GEISHA'S GRANDDAUGHTER (Five Star Press)

THE MARRIAGE BED (G.P. Putnam)

A FORBIDDEN LOVE (Berkley)

STREAMS IN THE WILDERNESS (Yoseloff)

Verse:

SPARKS (Gefen)

SEEK HAVEN (Reconstructionist Press)

www.ingramcontent.com/pod-product-compliance
Lightning Source LLC
Chambersburg PA
CBHW020615310726
48979CB00008B/1489/J

* 9 7 8 0 5 9 5 4 9 5 2 9 0 *